LONE STAR COWBOY

Rance Cameron had ridden a horse before he could walk and had packed a gun since he was sixteen. He looked like a Texan, but he didn't consider himself one yet – he was still a stranger in a strange land. And like the new German immigrants, he had fled his homeland to escape almost certain death. . . .

The feud between the Camerons and McPhersons had started over a trivial matter, but it had been fought almost to the last man so far as the Camerons were concerned. Outnumbered, with only a handful of survivors left from the death and devastation that had happened, the Camerons had left – while they still could.

Rance Cameron, with no home ties, became a wanderer on the face of the earth.

LONE STAR COWBOY

Leslie Scott

This hardback edition 1998
by Chivers Press
by arrangement with
Golden West Literary Agency

Copyright © 1959 by Arcadia House
Copyright © renewed 1989 by Lily Scott
Copyright © 1998 by Lily Scott in the British
Commonwealth

ISBN 0 7540 8034 X

British Library Cataloguing in Publication Data available

Printed and bound in Great Britain by
Redwood Books, Trowbridge, Wiltshire

LONE STAR
COWBOY

CHAPTER I

Sitting his horse near the waterfront of Carl-shafen, later to be called Indianola, Rance Cameron watched the immigrants disembark. There were not very many of them; about thirty, he judged, the forerunners of thousands that would later clog the disease-ridden port and dot the prairie with their graves.

They were a rather motley lot—solid-looking middle-aged men, buxom *frauen* with billowing skirts and quaint, old-world bodices, stalwart younger men, a few children and several blonde girls of fragile prettiness. All, even the children, lugged bags and bundles that contained the few possessions they had been able to salvage when they had fled their homeland.

A common expression stamped the features of

all, Cameron thought, and he tried to analyze it. Not exactly fright, although it was akin to fright, but rather a startled bewilderment and loneliness.

Rance Cameron experienced a feeling of deep sympathy for these poor people set down in an alien land amid strangers. To sympathize, one must have undergone a similar experience, and Cameron felt that he had. He lounged easily in his big Mexican saddle in true Texas style. He had ridden a horse before he could walk. He wore a heavy gun, one of the newer pattern Colts, sagging against his thigh in Texas fashion. He had packed one since he was sixteen. His costume was the garb of the rangeland—faded bibless overalls, soft blue shirt with a vivid neckerchief looped around the collar, a broad-brimmed, battered hat, the conventional "J.B.," well scuffed half-boots of softly tanned leather. But Rance Cameron was not a Texan, nor did he consider himself one yet. This flat, heat-drenched land was not his land, and there were times when he longed for the thin, cool air of the western Virginia hills. He, too, was a stranger in a strange land. And this aroused his sympathies as he gazed at the milling immigrants.

These people, participants in the incipient German revolution, had fled their homeland to escape almost certain death. Well, he, too, had "fled" his homeland for that very reason.

A feud, starting over a trivial matter, had broken out between the Camerons and the McPhersons of Calvert Valley, a feud that devastated the valley and left gaunt and lonely fire-blackened chimneys standing where homes had formerly stood, and graves brown and bare till new grass grew. It was a bitter feud, such a feud as is possible only to men whose forbears were born and reared in the Scottish glens. A feud fought almost to "the last man" so far as the Camerons were concerned. For the Camerons were few, the McPhersons many. Finally a handful of survivors, young Rance Cameron among them, seeing that if they remained their extinction was inevitable, left Calvert Valley while they were still able. Men with families found new places to settle and establish homes, but Rance Cameron, with no home ties, became a wanderer on the face of the earth, finally ending up in the new Republic of Texas. Cameron knew horses and he knew cattle, so it was logical for him to turn to ranch work. The tricks of rope and branding iron were easily mastered, and now after seven years, during which he had covered a good part of Texas and made one trip into what is now New Mexico, he was as able a cowhand as the Lone Star could boast.

There were times when he chuckled a trifle wryly at the thought of a man with a considerably better than average education spending his life following a cow's tail. But it was a living! And he had no ambition.

So Rance Cameron could feel for the sad, bewildered people on the wharf who gazed apprehensively at the unfamiliar scene and wondered what the future held for them.

Abruptly Cameron's interest quickened a little. Two people had disengaged themselves from the group and were walking toward him.

> *When there passes by a woman with*
> *The West in her eyes, and a man*
> *With his back to the East!*

The girl was small, slender and beautifully formed. She had dark hair inclined to curl, astonishingly big eyes of so deep a blue as to appear black, a pert nose and vividly red lips above a determined-looking little white chin. Her walk was lithe, graceful. On her face was no hint of the bewildered expression that marked the features of the others; rather, instead, there was a touch of haughty reserve.

The man was nearly six feet in height and weighed a muscular hundred and eighty-five pounds; a blond giant with sea-blue eyes who looked as if he had just stepped from the deck of a Viking ship rather than from a dingy tramp schooner.

The pair paused beside Cameron's splendid blue moros. The girl glanced up at the big horse's rider and spoke.

"My good man," she said in unaccented English, "can you direct us to the home of *Herr* Rosenthal?"

Cameron's gray eyes narrowed a little. He replied shortly, jerking his thumb over his shoulder:

"Keep on following the trail and you can't miss it."

He glanced down, noted the fragile satin slippers on her little feet and added:

"But it's considerable of a walk." He hesitated, then said, "You are welcome to ride in front of me if you care to, and I'll take you there."

The man spoke, and his voice was crisply arrogant, his English precise, accented.

"You will walk and the lady will ride."

Cameron gazed at him a moment wonderingly, but his voice was quiet when he replied:

"Wouldn't work. Smoke would stand her on her head in that mud puddle over there if she tried to throw a leg across him."

The girl flushed. "I can ride," she said.

"Perhaps," Cameron conceded, "but not this horse. He—look out!" he roared.

The man had reached a hand toward the moros. Just in time Cameron tightened an iron grip on the bridle and the slashing teeth missed their mark.

The man recoiled, decidedly startled. "That is a vicious brute!" he exclaimed.

"No, he's not vicious," Cameron differed. "It's just that he allows no one other than myself to put a hand on him. If you had even an elementary knowledge of horses, you would know it."

The man flushed. "I am—was a cavalry officer," he snapped, "and I shall tell you—"

"Listen, mister," Cameron broke in, "you

seem to understand the English language, and perhaps you'll get the drift of what I am going to tell you. This is a bad country to throw your weight around. It won't get you anything except possibly six feet of earth; a little more, maybe, seeing as you are a tall man."

Cameron expected a hot retort, but instead a smile abruptly lighted the other's handsome face like a ray of sunshine.

"Sir," he said, "I spoke wrongly, but when one has been accustomed all one's life to give orders and have them obeyed," he sighed, "it is hard to break oneself of the habit. I meant no offense."

"None taken," Cameron answered lightly. "Well, which is it—does the lady ride in front of me or do you both walk? It's all one to me."

The girl spoke. "I'll ride," she said. "Johan, if you will—"

Rance Cameron acted on impulse. He swayed in the saddle, reached down. The next instant the girl was perched in front of him. Her breath drew in sharply, but she didn't speak; only stared straight in front of her with stormy blue eyes, her lips compressed. Glancing sideways at the man, Cameron surprised what was undoubtedly a grin twitching the corners of his finely formed mouth. All of a sudden he decided that he liked Johan.

There was no conversation during the course of the ride. The girl continued to stare straight ahead. Cameron accommodated Smoke's gait to Johan's stride, and the trip took some little time. Finally Rance pulled up in front of a small but comfortable-looking house set in a grove.

"Here you are," he announced, and swung the girl lightly to the ground. "I'm pretty sure you'll find Mrs. Rosenthal home. Papa Rosenthal, as we call him, will be at his store this time of day. I'll stop by and tell him he has company."

"We thank you," said Johan. The girl said nothing.

Cameron nodded, turned Smoke and sent him back toward the settlement at a slow walk. The girl gazed after him.

"Johan," she said, "it would seem we have come to a strange land and a strange people."

"Yes, Your Highness," Johan replied. "Here, I think, we will find hardship, privation, perhaps danger and—great kindness."

"Kindness?"

"Yes. We have just had an example of it.

There was no reason he should go out of his way to accompany us here and invite you to ride."

"He wasn't very gracious about it."

Johan removed his hat, and abruptly he looked much older. His broad forehead was lined, and his yellow hair was liberally sprinkled with gray.

"It is the nature of such men to hide their kindly impulses under a cloak of brusqueness," he replied judiciously. "I would say from his appearance that he is of Scotch descent, and the Scots are not a people given to effusiveness, although there is usually plenty of fire beneath the ice, as perhaps you realize, your mother being a Scotswoman. I wonder if *his* ancestors fled to this wild land to escape persecution."

"Not likely," the girl replied, with a sudden proud lift of her chin. "Nobody ever persecuted the Scots. It was tried a few times, but the wild Highlanders stormed down from their glens with their twelve-foot spears and their two-handed claymores and that was the end of persecution."

"True," agreed Johan. "A proud people and warlike. The soft life was never for them."

The girl nodded, and her eyes grew somber.

"I wonder what reception we will get in New Braunfels?" she remarked.

Johan looked grave. "It is difficult to say," he replied. "Prince Carl Zu Solms-Braunfels is an unpredictable man, and he did not love your father."

"I've often wondered why," said the girl. "Brothers should not hate."

"When two men desire the same woman, it is but natural that he who loses her does not love his successful rival," Johan observed dryly.

The girl's eyes widened. "You never told me that before."

"There was no reason to do so," Johan replied. "But now, Your Highness—"

"Oh, stop calling me Your Highness," she interrupted impatiently. "I am no longer the Princess of Auerswald. An empty title at best—a tiny principality with a puppet ruler, that no longer exists. Call me Mary, as you used to."

"That was when you were a small girl," Johan smiled.

"Well, I'm still a rather small girl," she retorted, "and as I said, I am no longer a princess, as doubtless the Prince of Solms-Braunfels will lose no time in remarking."

"But you must have a name," Johan protested.

"All right," she said. "My mother's name is good enough for me. Here I am Mary Stewart, plain and unvarnished. I like it better than Auerswald, anyhow. Remember, I was educated in England and spent most of my girlhood days there and in Scotland. The land of Almain means little more to me than this. Why, I can't even speak the language decently, scarcely better than the Gaelic, and goodness knows I have little enough of that."

Johan smiled sadly. "So be it," he said. "I will try to remember."

The girl was still gazing after the departing horseman, now small in the distance.

"I wonder who and what he is," she remarked inconsequentially.

"It is difficult to say," Johan replied. "He may be nothing, or anything, for here all are equal. Or he may aspire to anything and realize his ambitions," he added reflectively. "Here there is also equal opportunity for all. Here a man is not fixed in the station to which he was born, as across the sea; he can aspire to anything. He who is nothing today sits in the seats of the mighty tomorrow. Aye, a strange land. Sometimes I wonder if what seemed dire calamity may not turn out to be but the beginning of the upward spin of Fate's wheel. Ha! there is the good *Frau* Rosenthal peering out of the window. From her, at least, we will receive a warm welcome."

CHAPTER II

Cameron pulled up in front of Rosenthal's store. Ezekiel Rosenthal—everybody called him Papa Rosenthal—had built his trail-end general store long before there was any Carlshafen. For years he had supplied the ranches for many miles around. Everybody liked and respected him. Cameron knew that Rosenthal took an active interest in the projected rehabilitation of German refugees.

Papa was out somewhere at the moment, so Cameron left his message with a clerk and rode on to John Rafferty's Best Chance Saloon.

Cameron hitched Smoke at a convenient rack and entered the saloon. It was late afternoon, and only a few customers, mostly cowhands, were lounging about. Cameron made his way to the far end of the bar where Rafferty was standing.

John Rafferty was a wondrously fat man with a handlebar mustache, and a spit curl plastered down over his forehead. He was jovial, kindly but a devil when aroused, his fatness being highly deceptive, as more than one badly bruised and battered gentleman had learned to his sorrow.

"Hello, Rance," he greeted the cowboy. "Understand you quit the Walking R."

"That's right, John," Cameron replied.

"How come? I always figured Rivercomb was a good man to work for."

"He is," Cameron said. "None better. I just got tired of staying in one place and figured it was time to trail my twine. I was with the Walking R nearly a year, you know."

Rafferty shook his head. "You'll end up a chuck-line rider," he predicted. "Stop at a ranch for a meal, dig a few post holes to pay for it and get tobacco money, and off again."

"Sort of a tramp on horseback," Cameron smiled.

"Sort of," Rafferty conceded. "But those fellers seem to have a good time; always happy, always looking to see what's over the next hill, never expecting to find it, whatever it is, and not giving a hoot anyhow."

Cameron chuckled; he felt Rafferty had stated his own case precisely.

The saloonkeeper's gaze was fixed on Cameron's holster. "Let's have a look at that new gun you got," he requested. "One of Sam Colt's latest models, isn't it?"

"That's right," Cameron said, drawing the iron and handing it to Rafferty. "It's a lot different from the old 'Texas,' his first gun. You know the barrel of the Texas had to be taken off to allow the empty cylinder to be replaced with a full one, and a man on horseback and going places would have a heck of a time holding those three parts. Also, the calibre was too light—.34, and with a four-and-one-half-inch barrel. Now this one is .44, with a nine-inch barrel. Plenty of weight and perfect balance. And look at this neat little lever rammer attached below the barrel; it accurately seats the bullets in the chamber without removing the cylinder. You can load this one in the saddle with the horse swallowing his head at midnight."

"She's a beauty, all right," Rafferty admitted admiringly. "Understand the Texas Rangers pack 'em."

"They do," Cameron said. "In fact, Ranger Captain Sam Walker is due about as much credit for this iron as Colt, for he met Colt in New York when he went there to buy arms for the republic, and together they worked out this gun that's called the Walker Colt. I understand Colt is working on still another model that will load from the back, using metal cartridges. That'll be a *gun*."

Rafferty chuckled at the younger man's enthusiasm. "Sort of hipped on guns, aren't you, Rance?" he observed.

Cameron grinned a trifle shame-facedly, for he was not as a rule given to enthusiasm of any kind. "The darn things have always held a certain fascination for me," he admitted. Abruptly his expression became stern. "But I haven't used one for quite a spell now, and I hope I'll never have to again," he added.

Rafferty nodded sympathetically. "Understand you handle one mighty fast and shoot mighty straight," he remarked.

"In the western Virginia hill country you learn to do both at an early age," Cameron replied grimly.

He was silent a moment, then continued. "John," he said, "this gun is going to bring about some changes that neither Colt nor Walker figured on. It's already changed the Rangers' method of fighting the Indians and the Mexicans. For the first time they're fighting them on horseback. Formerly the Indians with their arrows and, to a lesser degree, the Mexicans with their lances, had all the best of it when mounted. The Indians can shoot their arrows on horseback, fast and accurate, one after another, and a lance is a deadly weapon against an empty gun. Now things are different. With six shots at his command, the Ranger, armed with this gun, has the advantage. Before, they always dismounted to meet a charge and fired by platoons. Now they can go right after the hellions and keep on shooting. And I predict that before long there will develop a new type of gunfighter in the West— a man who can draw his gun fast and accurately get in his shots one after another. He'll no longer have to depend on the first shot, being able to shoot again and again and again. And he'll do even better with the new one Colt is working on. You watch and see."

Rafferty chuckled. "Bet you've already been

practicing it," he said.

Cameron grinned, and flushed a little. "Well, I have," he admitted. "But I told you I don't ever want to have to use one again. Let's have a drink!"

Rafferty toyed with his glass, gazing straight in front of him. He spoke without turning his head.

"Speaking of not wanting to use a gun again, you sure that isn't your real reason for trailing your twine?"

"What do you mean?" Cameron asked, although he knew very well what the saloonkeeper meant.

"I mean Lije Fitch," Rafferty said, still gazing to the front.

Cameron was slow in answering. Finally:

"John, you may be right. I've had enough of feuds to last me a lifetime; I don't desire to get mixed up in another."

"And you figure if you stay here you can't keep out?"

"I'd be working for the Walking R, wouldn't I?" Cameron countered. "Besides, there's a personal issue involved. Lije Fitch tried to get me to go to work for him when I first came here, as a guard for his wagon trains. I told him I didn't care for that kind of money. Guess it didn't set well with him. He's had no use for me since and makes it plain whenever he gets a chance. So far I've managed to avoid him, but there's a limit."

"You mean you didn't care to get mixed up in the smuggling business his trains are said to handle?"

"That's right," Cameron answered. "I know smuggling is regarded rather tolerantly down here, but just the same it is outside the law. I've been outside the law enough; I prefer to stay inside for a while."

Rafferty nodded. "And there are folks who think Fitch's Flying W herd grows mighty fast," he remarked with apparent irrelevancy.

"Including Jim Rivercomb of the Walking R," Cameron added dryly.

Rafferty nodded again. "Maybe you are doing the smart thing to pull out," he said. "No sense getting mixed up in a range war if you don't have to; they're as bad as your hill country feuds."

Cameron did not reply, and Rafferty changed the subject.

"Saw you were sort of consorting with the

Dutchies," he remarked.

"A couple of them wanted to know how to get to Papa Rosenthal's house, and I showed them the way," Cameron explained.

"A nice-looking girl," Rafferty commented.

"She'll pass," Cameron replied.

"What about the feller with her?"

"He's okay," Cameron said. "I like him. He'll make out."

"And the girl won't?"

"I didn't say that," Cameron demurred. "But she's got a lot to learn, and I'm afraid it's a hard country for her sort."

"Be hard on all of 'em," Rafferty predicted. "This little bunch should do all right. I hear they're going right on to that town of New Braunfels the crazy prince feller built on the land on the Comal River he bought from the Garzas of San Antonio. And I understand there are thousands more headed this way. This shack town ain't got accommodations for such a number, and with a war right around the corner, transportation is likely to be hard to find. They're liable to get bogged down here and have a tough time of it."

"Who's handling the arrangements for accommodations and transportation?" Cameron asked.

Rafferty ordered another drink and looked contemplative.

"Well," he said, "that prince feller, Carl Zu Solms-Braunfels, is commissioner-general for an outfit called the Society for the Protection of German Immigrants in Texas. I understand it's made up of German bigwigs, all noblemen, who figure to place a lot of refugees here and build up a big colony. The authorities over at the capital are in favor of it, naturally; what Texas needs more than anything else right now is people, and they figure most of the folks they get will be all right. Chances are they will be, if they can make out. No matter what happens to the prince and the bunch of store dudes he's got with him, I figure that town is here to stay, especially when everybody knows it'll just be a month or so till Texas is part of the United States. Then they'll be American citizens, which is what all of 'em want to be in the first place. They founded that town last March 21st with two hundred folks. So much for New Braunfels. Here at Carlshafen the details are handled by a feller named Sterns —Mark Sterns. I reckon he's all right, but I don't like him. I know Papa Rosenthal don't either, and Papa Rosenthal don't miss many bets."

"You can say that double," Cameron agreed heartily. "It's a pity he isn't handling things; then they'd get somewhere."

"That's what a lot of folks think," Rafferty said, "but Sterns seems to have a stand-in with the prince feller who's the big skookum he-wolf of the pack and is his representative here."

Rafferty didn't seem able to keep off the subject of Lije Fitch.

"That hellion and some of his men are in town today, drinking at a place down the street," he observed. "I don't like that hombre; he's a trouble hunter if there ever was one. Wouldn't be surprised if they drop in here sooner or later; I'd be just as pleased if they stayed away."

Cameron nodded in silence. He, too, hoped Fitch and his men would not visit the Best Chance. Sparks were liable to fly any time they got together, and Cameron was definitely not looking for trouble.

He was doomed to disappointment, however. A short time later Fitch and two companions swaggered into the saloon, and it was plain to see that they had been drinking heavily.

Fitch was a big square-shouldered man with intolerant black eyes, a tight, thin-lipped mouth and a long blue chin. He was aggressively handsome and had a reputation for having a way with women. He and his mates bellied up to the bar and demanded whiskey, which a bartender served without comment. Rafferty kept a watchful eye on the trio. Three heads drew together; and Cameron knew very well he was under discussion. Finally Fitch detached himself from the group and strode to where Cameron stood.

"Howdy, Mister Cameron," he said. "Understand you're pulling out of the section. A good notion; it *is* getting a bit crowded, for some kinds of people." The way he said it was a deliberate insult.

Cameron hit him dispassionately, but with all his weight behind his fist. Fitch hit the floor. He scrambled to his feet shouting curses, a big horse pistol in his hand, and John Rafferty realized that Cameron hadn't been fooling when he admitted he'd practiced drawing that new-fangled Colt from its sheath. Before Fitch could raise the pistol he found himself looking into a black muzzle. Cameron spoke quietly.

"Fitch, I don't want to kill you, but if you

don't behave yourself, I will," he said. "Drop that iron!"

Fitch continued to curse, but he let the pistol fall. At the same instant the muzzle of the Colt twitched sideways and gushed smoke. The hanging lamps jumped to the boom of the report.

One of Fitch's companions howled with pain and doubled up, gripping his bloody hand between his knees. A second pistol clattered to the floor. Cameron spoke again, still quietly.

"If this keeps up I *will* have to kill somebody. Get out, the lot of you, before I do! Pick up your pistol, Ftich, but keep the muzzle down. Don't be afraid; I won't shoot you in the back."

"Which is more than you could say for him," growled Rafferty as he took a Sharps buffalo gun from a rack behind the bar and cocked it. He followed the discomfited trio to the door, Fitch still cursing, the wounded man lurching and moaning. He watched them go down the street and out of sight. After making sure they were gone and not returning, he went back to where Cameron stood and laid the cocked Sharps on the bar.

"Let's see you load that thing, Rance," he requested interestedly. "Say! That's neat, ain't it!

Didn't take you half a minute, cap and all. And now what?"

"Now I think I'll have something to eat," Cameron replied as he holstered the Colt.

"A good idea," said Rafferty, "and I'll just keep the Sharps handy in case those hellions might take a notion to come back. I don't think they will, though; figure they got a bellyful for the time being. Seems you had to use one again, after all."

"Yes," Cameron agreed gloomily. "Time for me to pull out."

Cameron had finished his dinner and was enjoying a smoke when a young man came in, glanced about and hurried across to his table.

"Mr. Cameron," he said, "Papa Rosenthal told me to ask you to come up to the house for a little while."

"Okay," Cameron replied, pinching out his cigarette. "I'll come as soon as I feed my horse."

"Keep your eyes open," Rafferty warned as Cameron left the saloon. Cameron nodded but did not otherwise reply.

Twilight was deepening into night by the time Smoke finished his repast. Cameron mounted him and rode slowly to the Rosenthal house.

Mrs. Rosenthal, plump, bustling and motherly, ushered him into the living room, where he found Papa, Johan and the girl engaged in conversation. Papa Rosenthal was also on the rolypoly side, with shrewd twinkling brown eyes and a smiling mouth. He greeted Cameron warmly.

"Mary, this is Rance Cameron," he said to the girl. "Rance, this is Miss Stewart and *Herr* Johan Myerson."

The girl inclined her head the merest trifle.

"Mr. Cameron and I have met before, I believe," she said coolly.

Cameron looked blank. "We have?" he exclaimed. "Oh, yes, I remember now. You're the girl I packed up here this afternoon. Sorry! I'd forgotten."

He turned to shake hands with Johan, while Mary Stewart glared. Cameron sensed that Johan was again struggling to keep a grin under control. Papa Rosenthal looked a bit puzzled, but apparently thought it best to let the matter pass without comment.

"Rance," he said, "I understand you've quit the Walking R." Cameron nodded.

"And are sort of at loose ends right now?"

"That's right," Cameron admitted.

"Well," said Rosenthal, "I'm offering you a job."

"I'm leaving the section," Cameron replied briefly.

"The one I'm offering will take you away from the section," Papa Rosenthal countered.

Cameron grew interested. "Yes? How's that?"

"I'm sending Miss Stewart and *Herr* Myerson on to New Braunfels in one of my wagons," Papa Rosenthal explained. "I'd like for you to go along on the trip, to sort of keep an eye on things, as it were. It's a rough country between here and New Braunfels."

Cameron hesitated. He didn't particularly relish the idea of a two-hundred-mile trip in the snippy girl's company, but the look of wistful appeal in Johan's fine eyes decided him.

"Okay," he said. "I'll take it. Might as well be doing that as anything, and it'll give me a head start west. What about the rest of the bunch that came in on the ship?"

Papa Rosenthal's kindly face seemed to harden. "They will leave later," he said. "Mark Sterns has arranged for Lije Fitch to transport them in his freight wagons."

Papa did not elaborate, but Cameron saw

plainly that he was not pleased with the arrangement.

"What time do you figure to roll?" he asked as he stood up to go.

"About eight o'clock, if you can make it," Rosenthal replied.

"I can make it in twenty minutes," Cameron said. "See you in the morning."

Johan shook hands again. The girl nodded shortly but did not speak.

Again Rance Cameron rode back to town in a bad temper. He was annoyed with himself for allowing that confounded girl to irritate him. To all appearances she had taken a violent dislike to him, perhaps because he didn't kowtow to her. Rance Cameron had an American prejudice against kowtowing and saw no reason he should, to her or anybody else.

He dismounted in front of the Best Chance.

Rafferty looked expectant, so Cameron regaled him with an account of what had happened, adding his opinion that while Johan appeared to be all right, the girl was liable to prove a nuisance on the trip.

The wise old saloonkeeper shot him a shrewd glance and stroked his mustache. Then he delivered himself of an opinion that startled Cameron.

"Rance," he said, "I've a notion you ain't going to leave the section, after all."

"Not going to leave!" Cameron exclaimed. "Why, I'm pulling out tomorrow."

"Uh-huh, but you won't get any farther than New Braunfels," Rafferty predicted.

"Now what the devil do you mean by that?" Cameron demanded.

"You'll find out," Rafferty replied cheerfully. "Let's have a drink."

Rafferty downed his whiskey and departed to attend to his numerous duties. A little later, however, he was back. "Fitch and his two hellions rode out of town a little while ago," he announced. "The one you plugged had his hand tied up and in a sling, but I don't think he was hurt much. Watch out for Fitch, son; he won't forget, and he's bad."

"I don't think he'll folow me clean across Texas," Cameron replied.

"New Braunfels is less than a hundred and eighty miles from here, and that ain't far in Texas," Rafferty retorted significantly.

"Oh, this time next week I'll be way west of

New Braunfels," Cameron declared.

"Wanta bet?" Rafferty asked, and hurried off without waiting for a reply.

Cameron hung around the Best Chance for a while, then stabled Smoke and went to bed in a little room over the stalls.

CHAPTER III

When Cameron arrived at Papa Rosenthal's house the following morning he found the light covered wagon hitched up and ready to go. The girl sat on a seat under the protecting awning, but Johan was mounted, sitting his horse like a centaur. Cameron noted that he wore a brace of pistols. The wagon driver had a Sharps rifle resting against the seat beside him.

Cameron was forced to register grudging approval of the girl's costume. She wore a soft, mannishly cut shirt, open at the throat, and bibless overalls, later to be known throughout cow country as "Levis," probably advised and provided by Papa Rosenthal. Trim little riding boots had replaced the satin slippers, and a man's broad-brimmed hat perched jauntily on her dark curls.

Papa Rosenthal saw them off. He shook hands with Cameron and said in low tones, "Take care of them, Rance; they're good people and lonely."

Cameron promised the old man he'd do the best he could, but he felt that Papa's concern was hardly warranted. They would pass over a stretch of rough country, but all in all it was fairly civilized. There were outlaw bands in the hills, but an immigrant wagon was hardly likely to tempt them.

As he mounted Smoke, Papa drew near and said in a low voice, "I slipped something into your saddle pouch, Rance."

"What?" Cameron asked.

"Another Colt gun like the one you're wearing," Papa replied. "It's all loaded and ready to shoot."

"But why?" Cameron wanted to know.

"Because if you happen to need 'em, twelve shots are better than six," Papa replied sententiously.

"Well, thanks. It's a nice gift, but I really don't see why you think I should need it," Cameron said.

"Never can tell," Papa said, "never can tell. Hope to see you again soon."

"You're not likely to for quite a while," Cameron answered. "I'm heading back west."

Papa Rosenthal smiled, and somehow his smile was reminiscent of John Rafferty's answer to a similar declaration. Cameron growled under his breath, then flashed a grin at Papa and rode after the wagon, which was already under way.

The wagon was not heavily laden. Its load consisted of necessary provisions and cooking utensils, a light cot for the girl, blankets for the men and two small trunks.

A little later in the day, Cameron was riding beside Johan when the German spoke in his precise English.

"*Herr* Cameron," he said, "there is something I must tell you, something *Herr* Rosenthal advised me to tell you. In those trunks there is much gold."

"Gold?"

"Yes. It is consigned to Prince Carl from Baron von Meusebach who, it is said, will later replace the prince here."

Cameron whistled under his breath. "And does anyone other than Papa Rosenthal know of its existence?" he asked.

Johan hesitated, then spoke slowly.

"I think," he said, "that the *Herr* Mark Sterns knows of it. He is the prince's representative, and it is logical to assume that he does."

Cameron nodded, his eyes thoughtful. He glanced at Johan's armament.

"I suppose you know how to use those guns," he remarked.

"I can shoot, and from horseback; all cavalrymen can," Johan replied.

"Okay," Cameron said. "And the driver knows how to handle that old Sharps. I doubt if anything will happen, but just the same we must be prepared against such an eventuality. I wish we didn't have that girl along. A woman is an added responsibility and a handicap under such circumstances."

Johan smiled a little. "I think you will find that Her—that Miss Stewart will prove neither a burden nor a liability," he replied.

"I hope so," Cameron said without conviction. "Oh, well, no use bothering our heads about what might happen until and if it does happen." They rode on together.

All day Cameron kept a close watch on their

surroundings. The trail ran mostly across level pasture lands dotted with clumps of thicket and groves and with occasional low rises. However, the day and the night passed without incident.

When the trip was resumed the following morning, the country began to change. There were more low hills, thickly brush grown, an increase in the ever present chaparral growth. Cameron intensified his vigilance, for they were entering the wilder land south and east of Victoria.

After a noonday halt for food and to water the horses, the girl approached Johan and Cameron.

"Johan," she said, "would you mind if I rode the horse for a while?"

Myerson glanced questioningly at Cameron before replying.

"Oh, let her ride," Cameron conceded indifferently. "She'll get her nose sunburned and it'll peel, but nothing worse, I reckon. She should be able to sit that old plug."

There was a slight sound, as if small white teeth were ground together, but otherwise Miss Stewart did not comment. She waited till Cameron and Johan shortened the stirrup straps and then mounted without assistance. Cameron was surprised to see that her seat was easy and lounging, in contrast to Johan's rather stiff cavalry stance. He wondered where she had learned to ride. Without speaking, he reined in beside her and they preceded the wagon. She gazed straight ahead of her and was apparently oblivious to his existence. A little later, however, she made a remark that caused him to realize she was more observant than he had thought.

"Mr. Cameron," she said, "you seem to be studying the country all the time, as if you were expecting something. Do you think there is a chance someone has designs on the gold?"

Cameron shrugged his broad shoulders. "Not beyond the realm of possibility," he admitted. "This is a country where anything is liable to happen and sooner or later usually does.

"I can't understand why they didn't send it with the main train," he added. "That must consist of several wagons with armed drivers."

"I don't, either," she agreed, "but Mr. Rosenthal seemed to think it best that we take it with us. It is in the charge of Johan, you know."

Cameron nodded. At the moment he didn't care to discuss the matter. The girl seemed to hesitate; then she spoke again.

"After you agreed to accompany us on the journey, Mr. Rosenthal insisted that we take the gold," she added. "He seemed to think that with you along it would be perfectly safe."

"Nice of him," Cameron replied dryly. "I hope his confidence isn't misplaced."

The blue eyes glinted sideways at him. "I don't think it is," she said quietly, and for the first time he saw her smile slightly, a shadowy smile that seemed to end almost before it began. He abruptly decided that with enough provocation she might actually become human.

They rode on in silence, the wagon lumbering after them. Cameron made no attempt to draw her into conversation. If she wanted to talk, okay, but he did not intend to invite a rebuff by what she might construe as undue familiarity on the part of a mere hired hand. Besides, his attention was occupied with the country ahead, particularly the long, gentle and thickly brush-grown slope on their right, which rolled upward to a rounded crest fully a thousand yards distant.

On the slope some four hundred yards above where they rode, a horseman materialized from the brush, reined up in a little cleared space, and sat gazing toward the trail. He made a striking picture, silhouetted against the background of gray-green chaparral, the fierce blaze of the afternoon sun outlining every detail of dingy white turban, single eagle feather set slantwise in the hair, necklace of bear's claws, loincloth and high boot-moccasins. Perfectly motionless he sat, a rifle resting in the crook of his arm.

"Why, it's an Indian, isn't it?" said the girl.

"No, it is not an Indian," Cameron replied, his eyes fixed on the distant figure. As he spoke, the horseman wheeled his horse and disappeared in the brush.

"Not an Indian!" she exclaimed. "Why, he looked just like pictures I've seen."

"No, he is not an Indian," Cameron repeated. "He's some jigger masquerading as an Indian. He did a pretty good job, too, but he slipped up on a couple of details. He wore a turban with an eagle feather slanting over his ear. No Eastern Plains Indian—and that's all we've got here—ever wore such a thing. That jigger, whoever he is, has had experience with Indians in southwest Texas or even farther west. That was an Apache get-up, and there are no Apaches here. Now what the blazes is the meaning of this? Why such a get-up? And why did he ride into plain view like he did, as if he wanted us to get a good look at him?"

The questions were directed at himself rather than at the girl, who looked bewildered. Cameron, however, did not elaborate. He fell silent, his whole attention fixed on the shadowy slope.

The girl was quiet for a moment; then she said, "You certainly have a wonderful eye for detail. All I noticed in the man's get-up was the general effect."

Cameron smiled slightly. "If you want to stay alive in this corner of the world, you have to learn," he replied.

"Am I to take that as advice?" she asked. He countered with a question of his own:

"Do you figure to stay here?"

She answered simply, "Yes," and glanced at him expectantly. Cameron felt that she desired to continue the discussion.

"Well," he said, "I hope you won't consider me presumptuous, but I am venturing to advise you, in a way. It is a wild land and a rough land. As a rule, a woman receives the greatest consideration, but the rule is not infrangible. There are some people to whom nothing is sacrosanct, and the ability to recognize such comes in handy sometimes, just as a developed instinct for a situation and its possible significance is of value."

"As you read significance into what happened a little while ago," she said slowly. She turned in her saddle to face him. "Mr. Cameron," she said, "you have an unusual way of expressing yourself for—" She hesitated.

"For a hired hand," he smilingly finished.

"I didn't intend to say any such thing," she retorted, a hint of exasperation in her voice. "I meant to say for a man who lives in what you yourself characterized as a wild and rough land."

"Most who live here came from elsewhere," he replied. "Yourself, for example."

"Yes, I guess that is so," she agreed. "I wonder why they come?"

"Some to forget the past, some with an eye to the future, more, I would say, because of the spirit of restlessness with which the Anglo-Norman and the Gael are imbued."

"You are of Scottish descent," she stated rather than asked.

"Partly," he conceded.

"My mother was Scottish."

"So I gathered. And your father?"

"He was a German nobleman, the former ruler of a little principality about the size, I would judge, of one of your Texas cattle ranches."

"And you chose to take your mother's name rather than the title to which you have a right?"

"As I understand, in America princes and princesses do not exist," she replied.

"The titles do not exist," he corrected her.

"Then in America one can aspire to nobility?"

"Nobility of the spirit, perhaps."

"The only true nobility," she said. Suddenly she laughed aloud, and he was actually startled by the metamorphosis of her expression.

"We're getting on, aren't we?" she said, her big eyes dancing.

"A lot better than I expected," he admitted.

"You are thinking of our first meeting, I suppose," she observed. "Well, I'm human, although you may not believe I am, and right then I was not in the best of tempers. I had just completed an exhausting sea voyage and had been dumped like so much cargo into a land not of my choosing. My future appeared anything but promising, and I was rebellious against the intrigue that was responsible for my being here. I knew

I didn't look my best, which is enough to do unpleasant things to any woman's disposition. I hadn't, and still haven't for that matter, any notion as to just what would be my reception in New Braunfels from my uncle, Prince Carl, who is a most unpredictable person, especially if I refuse to go along with his plans for me. It is a woman's prerogative, you know, to change her mind, and in the course of the trip across the Atlantic I changed mine a number of times and felt that when I reached New Braunfels I would very likely change it again. All of which did not make for an equable outlook on the world in which I found myself. And *you*! From the lofty eminence of your great horse you surveyed me most superciliously, and I felt that you were silently laughing at me, which was even worse. So I decided to take you down a peg and proceeded to try to do so. I fear, however," she admitted frankly, "that I didn't get very far.

"You seemed a rather terrible person at first, and very masterful," she added. "And a woman always resents a man being too masterful—at first."

"And later?"

"Oh, if she's a wise woman she lets him keep

on thinking he is."

It was Cameron's turn to laugh. "Especially if she is or was a princess and accustomed to giving orders and having them obeyed."

"Oh, a woman doesn't have to be a princess to get her orders obeyed, if she is smart enough to make them appear a request or an entreaty," she returned lightly.

Cameron experienced a slightly bewildered feeling that he was getting exactly nowhere in this game of repartee. As he endeavored to marshal his somewhat disordered faculties, a shout sounded behind them. The horses had been allowed to choose their own gait, and the wagon was catching up.

"Did you see the Injun back there a ways?" the driver called.

"Yes, I saw him, Bert," Cameron said.

"Think there's a bunch back in the brush figuring to raid us?"

"I don't think we have to worry much about an Indian raid," Cameron replied enigmatically. "About all we have left here are Coahuiltecans and a few Tonkawas, neither of whom are particularly hostile people and not much given to raiding."

"Maybe not," replied Bert, "but just the same I aim to be keeping my eyes skun along toward morning, when they'll hit us if they figure to. I don't trust any of the red devils."

Cameron nodded without comment.

CHAPTER IV

It was an hour before sunset when Cameron called a halt for the night. They had reached a spot he considered favorable to his plan of defense against a possible raid. It was a small clearing through which the trail ran. To the right was a wall of dense chaparral growth a hundred yards distant and on the far side of a little stream. To the left was a gentle slope, fairly well brush-grown, the bush thinning a bit toward the western terminus of the clearing. Here Cameron ordered the wagon halted.

"A bit early, but it's a good spot, and we might not find another farther on," he explained to his companions.

Cameron was silent during the evening meal. He knew the girl was studying him, but she asked no questions and proffered no comment. As the lovely blue dusk began sifting down from the hilltops like impalpable dust, Cameron drew Johan and Bert, the driver, aside.

"Tonight you don't spread your blankets under the wagon, as usual," he told them. "Wait till it's a bit darker and then take them up on the slope opposite the wagon, a score or so paces."

"But, Rance, if the red devils are figuring to pull something, they won't do it till around daylight," protested Bert.

"Yes, but as it happens, I'm not expecting a raid by Indians, if there happens to be one," Cameron explained. He briefly recounted his penetration of the horseman's disguise.

"Danged if you ain't right, feller!" exclaimed Bert. "Now you mention it, that *was* an Apache get-up, and there ain't no Apaches here. And the hellion rode out so we'd get a good look at him and figure he was an Injun."

"Exactly," Cameron replied.

"But why?" asked the puzzled driver.

"Two reasons, I'd say," Cameron answered. "First, to lull us into a sense of false security during the early part of the night. Second, if somebody managed to escape—and I really doubt they'd kill the girl except by accident—the report would be that the wagon was raided by Indians, which would be to the advantage of somebody with such a scheme in mind."

"Uh-huh, I can see that," Bert agreed. "Folks would be looking for Injuns, and the real hellions wouldn't even be suspected."

"Exactly," Cameron repeated. "Well, we might as well start moving. I'll spread my bed a little farther down the trail. I figure that if an attempt is made, the real try will be for the wagon, and it'll be from this side and farther down. They could diagonal from the thick brush down there and reach the wagon easily if our attention was centered on a false attack from across the creek."

"That's right," agreed Bert. "This is liable to be fun."

"May not be so funny," Cameron countered grimly. "If I'm right in what I'm thinking, we're up against a bad bunch with plenty of savvy. Don't take any chances."

As he spread his blankets, Cameron wondered how to get the girl out of the wagon without unduly alarming her. He supposed he'd have to ask Johan to lend a hand. However, that proved unnecessary. He had just straightened up from the blankets when he saw a white figure approaching. It was the girl. She paused beside him, her face a blur in the deepening dusk.

"Mr. Cameron," she said, "you expect trouble, do you not?"

"I'm taking precautions against such a possibility," he admitted. "I'm glad you showed up, for I wanted to tell you not to sleep in the wagon tonight. Go up on the slope where Johan and Bert are."

She did not answer for a moment; then she said, "I think I'll do very well right here."

"But here is close to any row that may break loose," he protested.

"You're staying here," she pointed out.

"Yes, but—" he began.

"So I'm staying right here, too," she interrupted cheerfully but firmly. "If you can risk your life to protect strangers, I see no reason why—"

It was his turn to interrupt. "But I don't consider you strangers any more," he exploded.

"All the more reason why I should stay," she countered, dropping down on the blanket and gazing up at him through the deepening gloom.

"Oh, well, I suppose there's no use arguing

with you." He sighed resignedly. "Only for Pete's sake if something does break loose, hug the ground; flying lead doesn't play any favorites."

"You might as well be comfortable," she said, patting the blanket beside her. "There, that's better. You don't look so stern sitting down, or so masterful."

"I begin to believe you have a very reprehensible sense of humor," he observed disgustedly. "You appear to take a sadistic pleasure in poking fun at me."

"Really I wasn't," she protested. "I was just stating an obvious fact."

"That's even worse," he growled. "It seems you also have a not at all commendable genius for cutting a man down."

"It's necessary at times," she returned. "Otherwise he's liable to become impossible."

"Impossible for what?"

"Impossible to live with."

He turned to stare at her, or to try to through the blackness.

"And I still have several days of living with you, as it were, do I not?" she asked innocently.

They both fell silent. Overhead, the bonfire

stars of Texas blazed in a sky of blue-black velvet. A little wind wandered through the tree tops, whispering to the leaves, as if wondering where to go and unable to make up its mind. The nearby brook prattled mischievously over its stones and seemed to chuckle to itself over some outlandish joke known only to brooks. A night bird called, and a daytime compatriot cheeped a sleepy protest. From the farther distance came the lonely, hautingly beautiful plaint of a hunting wolf. The girl spoke.

"Mr. Cameron," she said softly, "I believe I'm going to like this country, after all."

"It is a rough land for a woman who has been gently reared."

"Not always so gently," she countered. "Scotland is also wild and rough, and I spent considerable time there. I liked it."

"Then perhaps you'll be able to stand it here," he conceded. "Wait a minute."

He deftly draped the second blanket around her shoulders as he spoke.

"No more talking above a whisper, now, and the less of that the better," he warned. "Sounds carry a long way on a still night. More comfortable?"

"Yes," she breathed, "but how about you?"

"I'm used to it," he whispered reply. "Keep quiet, now, and listen."

The small wind was dying down and the night was very still. There was no moon, but the brilliant stars cast a faint and silvery sheen over the open space and outlined the white bulk of the wagon. The stand of brush on the far side of the stream was a solid wall of blackness. The thinner growth directly ahead showed paler patches. As the minutes dragged by, the silence remained unbroken.

It was a tedious vigil.

The night wore on, and Cameron guessed it must be getting along toward midnight. Still nothing moved in the shadows; no sound broke the stillness. And then abruptly he heard a smothered crackling in the brush somewhere ahead, as if a stealthily advancing foot had inadvertently trodden on a rotten stick. He tensed, listening for a repetition of the sound, which did not come.

And then without warning a hideous screeching yell sounded from the growth beyond the creek, and a stutter of gunfire. Bullets thudded into the ground under the wagon clanged against the tires.

The girl jumped and gasped. "Thought so," Cameron muttered, and shoved her roughly down on the ground. "Stay there and don't move," he ordered. In another instant he was gliding forward in the shadow of the growth. He had drawn his Colt and cocked it. The second gun, Papa Rosenthal's gift, was thrust under his belt on the left side.

The uproar across the creek continued, and bullets still hammered the ground under the wagon. Cameron ground his teeth; the murderous devils intended to show no mercy to the men of the party. Directly ahead, a score of yards distant, four more solid shadows disengaged from the brush and ran toward the wagon.

Cameron did not hesitate to shoot. The raiders intended robbery and murder, nothing less. He took deliberate aim and squeezed the trigger. The Colt banged, and the foremost runner pitched forward on his face. Cameron fired two more shots in quick succession. A second man spun around like a top and fell. Cameron heard the spiteful crack—one—two—of Johan's pistols, and a third man went down. Then Bert's buffalo gun let go with a thunderous boom, and the fifty-calibre slug seemed literally to blow the fourth man through the air to come down sprawling in the grass.

"Got him!" roared Bert.

For an instant it looked as if the fight were over; then from the brush beyond the creek burst five men. Weaving and ducking, they made for the wagon. Cameron fired his three remaining shots at the elusive targets and didn't score a hit. He holstered the empty gun and drew the second Colt, mentally blessing Papa Rosenthal for having provided it. He took careful aim at one of the figures, now almost to the creek bank, and pulled trigger. The outlaw plunged forward and lay still. Again the two pistols cracked, Johan having had time to reload, and again a man fell. The roar of the Sharps split the air, and a third raider was accounted for. Bullets fanned Cameron's face as the remaining outlaws answered the fire.

Two to go! Cameron took deliberate aim at the red flashes spurting toward him. As he pressed the trigger the world exploded in roaring flame and he pitched forward onto his face.

CHAPTER V

When Cameron regained consciousness he was lying beside the wagon, his head in the girl's lap, and she was sponging his forehead with a damp cloth. He looked up at her dazedly for a moment. In the glow of the lantern somebody had lighted, her face looked white and sick, her eyes great dark pools of shadow.

"Told you it was a rough country," he mumbled with a wan grin.

"It's a terrible country," she answered, her voice catching. "Are you all right?"

"I've got a sore head, but I'll be okay in a minute," he said, painfully struggling to a sitting position.

"Just a crease, feller," said Bert's cheerful voice. "Barely nicked the skin. Feeling better?"

"I'll be fine if somebody will get me a drink of water," Cameron replied. Johan hurried off to the creek and returned a moment later with a full pannikin. Cameron drank about a pint of it and felt much better.

"If you'll just give me a hand I believe I can stand up," he told Johan.

In answer, the tall German slipped an arm around his waist and lifted him to his feet as if he were a child. Cameron leaned against the comforting arm for a moment, then straightened up. The girl was anxiously hovering about him. He grinned at her cheerfully, then turned to Bert.

"How'd it end?" he asked.

"One got away," the driver answered. "After you downed his pardner, just before you tumbled over, he turned tail and cut back into the brush. Our guns were empty, and we had to let him go. Heard him tearing off at a gallop a minute later. Was quite a ruckus while it lasted. This clearing looks like the battle of the Alamo all over. Eight of the devils altogether, and nary an Injun among 'em; they'll make fine buzzard bait. We'll look 'em over closer in the morning and see if we know any of 'em. Now I'm going to get the fire going and heat us all some coffee—reckon we can use it. Then the rest of you can snooze a little till daylight. Me, I'm going to sit up with old Bellerin' Betsy in my lap, just in case. Don't worry about me; I can sleep on the wagon seat tomorrow. I've done it many a time."

Cameron felt too sick and exhausted to argue the point. After drinking the coffee, he allowed Mary Stewart to lead him to his blankets, on which he collapsed with a sigh of relief. When he was lying down, his head didn't ache quite so abominably.

"Johan, please bring my blankets from the wagon," Mary said. "No! I wouldn't sleep in that thing again for the world. I'm going to stay here beside Mr. Cameron to make sure he's all right."

Again Cameron didn't argue the point. Very quickly he fell into a sodden sleep.

The sun was shining brightly when he awoke.

"Breakfast is ready," Mary told him. "I insisted you be allowed to sleep as long as possible. How do you feel now?"

"A lot better," he replied, sitting up and knuckling his eyes. "My head's gotten back to something like its normal size. First time I ever got hit a wallop by a slug that way; hope it's the last time. You sleep well?"

"Wonderfully," she answered, coloring a little, "although right after that awful fight I thought I'd never be able to sleep again. I guess I'm getting used to the country."

"You'll end up a regular Texan," he chuckled, getting to his feet. "I'm going down and douse my head in the creek; I've a notion the cold water will do it good."

After breakfast Cameron and Bert examined the bodies of the slain raiders. They were typical of the plains and coastal area, but little more. Some looked hard, others didn't.

As they drew away from the others, Bert spoke in low tones.

"Rance," he said, "that little one with the busted nose—I'm sure I've seen him before, riding guard on a wagon train."

"Yes?"

"Uh-huh, and I reckon you've guessed it—one of Lije Fitch's trains."

Cameron nodded. "But it isn't right to hold Fitch responsible, even to suspect he is responsible for the acts of somebody he happened to hire," he pointed out. "No man can ever be perfectly sure of the people he hires."

"Reckon that's so," replied Bert in a voice that carried no conviction. "Just the same, you keep your eyes open if you happen to go back to the coast."

"I don't intend—" Cameron began, then left the sentence unfinished.

"Wonder what the wagon train following us will think when they hit this clearing—Fitch's wagon train—" Bert remarked with a chuckle.

"Let them think whatever they please," Cameron said. "When we reach Victoria, which we should before noon, we'll notify the authorities there, and they can send a sheriff or deputy to look them over and do what he sees fit. We certainly can't bury them, even if it was advisable."

"Right; let 'em lay here and rot," growled Bert. "And, Rance, if you hadn't sized up that Injun-looking one yesterday like you did, it would be us scattered around on the grass. The snake-blooded devils didn't figure to leave anybody alive, not even the girl, I bet."

CHAPTER VI

The wagon, proceeding slowly, reached Victoria shortly before noon. Cameron decided to lay over the rest of the day and the night.

"From here on we'll make faster time," he told Mary Stewart. "The trail is better and it's straighter. Up here from the coast it's as crooked as a snake in a cactus patch. Takes better than forty miles of going to cover an actual distance of thirty. You can sleep in a decent bed tonight for a change."

"I'd be perfectly content to sleep under the stars, but I could use a bath," she replied. "That is, if I can find one in this wild land of yours."

"I expect you can," he returned cheerfully. "Why didn't you say something this morning? I'd have doused you in the creek."

She glanced up at him through her lashes. "There were others present," she said. "And by the way, is my nose peeling?"

"It didn't even burn!" he snorted. "Not that even sunburn could appreciably detract from its perfection."

"Thank you, sir," she said demurely. "I'm glad you like—my nose, at least."

Cameron had no trouble finding accommodations for his party. Then he got in touch with the sheriff, who was in town, and regaled him with an account of the raid and its negative results.

The sheriff didn't appear overly impressed. "Always something busting loose in this section," he observed. "Glad you did for the no-good bums. I'll ride down and look 'em over later if I find the time. No matter, anyhow, just so long as they're accounted for. If the buzzards and coyotes eat 'em, they'll be doing so at their own risk of getting pizened."

After leaving the sheriff, Cameron repaired to a nearby saloon for a drink, which he felt he needed. Then he went to make sure that Smoke and the other horses were properly cared for. This chore taken care of, he wandered about the town a bit and hunted up Bert, whom he found in another saloon engaged in a session of poker with some more teamsters. There was a vacant chair, and Cameron spent several entertaining and slightly profitable hours with the pasteboards. Finally the effects of his largely sleepless night began to take toll, and he headed for the little hotel in which the party had secured accommodations. He mounted the stairs and was just entering his room near their head when the opposite door opened and Mary Stewart stood before him.

"Come in and talk awhile, Mr. Cameron," she said. "It's lonesome here with nothing to do, and I can't seem to get sleepy."

Cameron himself was suddenly very wide awake. He hesitated, then accepted the invitation.

"Sit down and be comfortable," she said, closing the door. "You can have the chair; I'll take the edge of the bed. They're frugal with furniture here."

Cameron obeyed, tossing his broad-brimmed hat aside and ruffling his thick black hair with slender bronzed fingers. The girl sat opposite him, crossed her knees, rested her round chin in one pink palm and proceeded to regard him during a silence that finally grew a bit embarrassing. Cameron racked his brains for some subject of conversation and at last hit on one he felt was safe.

"Miss Stewart, how did you happen to come to Texas?" he asked.

She continued to regard him a moment, then answered, "I was brought here to be married."

Cameron started, his eyes widening.

"To be married!"

"Yes," she said, "a marriage of convenience, engineered by my uncle, Prince Carl, for political reasons. Such things are cut and dried on the Continent, you know. His family is very rich and powerfully placed."

Cameron stared at her, nonplussed. "And do you intend to go through with it?" he asked impulsively.

Again she hesitated. "I really don't know," she said at length. "Such was my intention when I left Germany, but somehow things appear a little different four thousand miles away."

Cameron found himself floundering a bit. "Is your—the man distasteful to you?" he asked.

"Not at all," she replied. "He is—or was a very charming person."

Cameron felt he was getting more and more beyond his depth.

"Then why do you hesitate to marry him?" he asked.

This time she did not delay her reply. "Perhaps it is because of my Scottish ancestry, but I have always felt there is a certain ingredient essential to marriage."

"And what's that?" he asked.

"Love!"

"And you don't love him?"

She shrugged daintily. "I hardly know him. I haven't seen him for four years. I met him only once, when our betrothal was announced, after which he accompanied my uncle on a tour around the world and then came here to Texas where Prince Carl planned his German settlement."

"I see," Cameron said thoughtfully.

A dimple showed at the corner of her red mouth.

"You don't, not at all," she said, "but it doesn't matter. Mr. Cameron, were *you* ever in love?"

"Good Lord, no!" was his startled answer. "Why do you ask such a question?"

"I don't think you'd know it if you were," she

announced calmly.

"Why—why—" he sputtered. She went on, apparently heedless of his bewilderment.

"I wonder if the old Scottish covenantors weren't all like you," she said. "Repressed, rather stern, with square chins and cold eyes except for lights in their depths. Yes, I think they were. I think John Calvin himself must have been very like you."

Although he was in no mood for mirth, Cameron had to grin. He felt that the grim old reformer wouldn't have been flattered by the comparison.

"But I doubt if he could smile like that," she added. "It is unlikely that he was able to see much humor in anything. Which was a pity. A sense of humor is a saving grace. You are really rather attractive when you smile, Mr. Cameron."

"And *you* don't have to smile," he answered.

The dimple returned, more pronounced than before. "That was nicely put," she said. "But why are you so afraid of me, and apparently of nothing else that lives?"

"Afraid of you!"

"Yes," she replied. "If I said 'Boo!' real loud right now, I believe you'd jump out the window.

Wouldn't you?"

She stood up as he started to sputter an answer. Cameron also stood up.

Abruptly he picked up his hat, turned and strode out of the room, closing the door behind him.

CHAPTER VII

The evening of the fourth day from Victoria,
they reached the sprawling little settlement of
New Braunfels, dominated by its fort. On a high
hilltop where he could command a view of the
country for miles around, Prince Carl had built
his fort, which he called Sophienburg, and
where he lived in great style, surrounded by a
magnificence that amazed his neighbors, matter-
of-fact Texas pioneers. Lacking a German flag,
he raised the flag of Austria above the building.
The Texas flag was also raised.

With Cameron and Johan riding in front, the
wagon rolled up the hill to the fort, where considerable excitement at its approach was quickly
apparent. As it pulled to a halt, liveried lackeys
hurried out to unload the baggage and care for

the horses. An officer, glittering with gold lace, appeared. He bowed low to Mary and Johan and said something in German.

"He's telling us the prince awaits us," the girl whispered to Cameron. "Come; you will witness something amusing. Things are even more outlandish than I anticipated."

They followed the officer along a corridor and into a large hall. The rough stone walls were hung with rich tapestries, giving an air of considerable luxury. At the far end was a low dais upon which rested an elaborately carved and gilded chair. Around the dais were grouped a number of men and women resplendently garbed. In front of the dais stood a man dressed as for a state occasion.

"The prince," Mary said in low tones.

Prince Carl spoke in a sonorous voice. "Welcome, Maria!" he called. "Draw near, please." He acknowledged Johan's low bow with a nod, shot a questioning glance at Cameron.

The girl walked forward composedly, apparently oblivious to the comic opera surroundings. Johan followed, a pace to the rear. Cameron hung back a little.

Mary extended her hand, and the prince

bowed over it. The three engaged in low-voiced conversation, the prince listening intently to what the girl and Johan had to say.

Cameron, lounging easily a few paces back, studied him. Prince Carl was a fine-looking man, with dreamy eyes and a stubborn chin. Cameron could envision him leading a lost cause, wringing victory from defeat, and foregoing the fruits of victory to follow some other will-o'-the-wisp. Through his mind drifted Jacob's lament over Reuben, his wayward son: *"Unstable as water, thou shalt not excel!"*

No, Prince Carl would not last here; but he had planted a tree that would grow sturdily and in time spread far its branches.

Suddenly the prince raised his glance to Cameron, who stood regarding the scene with a tolerant amusement he managed to conceal. Carl strode forward with a winning smile, his hand outstretched, and spoke in English with barely a trace of accent.

"Herr Cameron," he said, "I am greatly in your debt, and my gratitude is profound. Were it not for your courage and resourcefulness, I would have lost not only the treasure, which is not small, but also, which is much more, Maria

and Johan. I repeat, I am greatly in your debt!"

He shook hands heartily, and Cameron felt that despite his stilted speech and his love of ornate display, there was nothing vapid or insincere about the man. He returned the prince's grip and smiled in return.

"After all, sir, my own life was sort of at stake," he deprecated the part he had played.

Prince Carl chuckled. "Ha! you Americans!" he exclaimed. "There is no stopping you. Some day you will rule the world."

"We're hardly a part of the world now, sir," Cameron smiled in reply.

"But soon you will be," Prince Carl declared with emphasis. "Your country is destined to be the world's greatest land, and I am proud to think that the descendants of my faithful followers here will play their own small part in her greatness. And now, as a slight token of my gratitude and appreciation, I wish to offer you my hospitality, such as it is, for as long as may be convenient to you.

"And I hope," he added, "that it will be for a very long time."

He searched the group of courtiers with his eyes and beckoned. A fresh-faced young man with smiling eyes came forward.

"Heinrich," said the prince, "you will conduct *Herr* Cameron to his quarters and see that his every wish is instantly met. I will speak with you again at dinner," he told Rance.

Cameron nodded his acceptance and followed the young officer. He turned for an instant, and his eyes met Mary's, which were dancing with what he decided was repressed mirth.

The room to which the officer led him was large and comfortably furnished, with a wide window that afforded a splendid view of the surrounding prairie. The officer closed the door and turned to Cameron with a grin.

"The prince chose me to escort you because I speak the language," he announced.

"You speak it as if you were born to it," Cameron commented.

"I was," Heinrich returned cheerfully. "I was born in Maryland. A few years back my parents returned to the old country. I accompanied them, but I didn't like it there, and when the prince offered me a berth with his expedition, I jumped at the chance. Now is there anything I can do for you?"

"I'd be glad if you'd fetch my saddle pouches,"

Cameron returned. "I've got a clean shirt and clean overalls and a razor in them."

Heinrich glanced at Cameron's garb with approval. "After a while, they'll get over this nonsense, and we'll be able to dress as befits the country," he said. "I don't think the prince will last much longer, or the crowd that surrounds him; they can't take it. But the solid people down below will remain."

"I understand there are more coming," Cameron observed.

"Yes, too many in too short a time," Heinrich replied. "Carlshafen, or Indianola, as people are already beginning to call it, hasn't the necessary accommodations, and I predict transportation to New Braunfels is going to pose a difficulty. Annexation to the United States is coming very shortly, and after that there'll be a war with Mexico in a few months, sure as shooting. Teamsters will be able to make big money transporting army supplies, and they'll break their contracts with the prince's representative. Watch and see if they don't. I fear the new arrivals are in for trouble and plenty of it."

"I've a notion you're right," Cameron agreed. "It looks like it, Heinrich."

"Call me Henry when the prince isn't around," the other interrupted. "He's a stickler for formality, and we have to humor him while he's here. Really it's all laughable, and a bit pathetic. He's living in a dream world, always has been and always will be. And he's stubborn as a mule when he has his head set on something, but he's a good man and kindly. He envisions a German principality here; he'll end up with a town."

"He could do worse."

"You're right," Henry agreed. "What Texas needs more than anything is good substantial communities. I'll fetch the pouches and everything else needful."

Cameron enjoyed a bath, a shave and clean clothes. Although he regarded his gun as much a part of his costume as his pants, he laid it aside for the evening. He was sitting by the window smoking when Henry tapped on the door again.

"Dinner will be served in five minutes," he said. "It is the custom to gather in the hall and await the coming of the prince. His habit is to make a grand entrance."

Together they descended the stairs to the hall, where a number of people were assembled. Standing to one side was Mary Stewart, conversing with a man.

He was a slender young man, but his slenderness, Cameron thought, was the steely slenderness of a rapier blade. He had blond hair, gay reckless blue eyes, and his features were almost cameo perfect.

And that, Cameron told himself with conviction, is the man she figures to marry.

He was right. Mary caught his eyes and beckoned him to approach.

"Mr. Cameron," she said, "allow me to present Count Otto von Salzburg." She glanced meaningly at him as she spoke.

Count Otto didn't appear to notice the form of the introduction, but Cameron did. She had presented the count to him, not him to the count, which was undoubtedly a breach of court etiquette. Cameron knew very well it was not a mistake on her part and wondered why she had done it.

The count shook hands with warmth and spoke in halting English with a thick accent.

"*Herr* Cameron," he said, "most pleased to meet you am I, and grateful, most grateful."

Cameron was forced to admit that this debonair stripling was charming despite the marks of dissipation that marred his comely features and the aura of wild recklessness that seemed to surround him. He could see Otto von Salzburg living a life that at its end would be recalled only "to point a moral and adorn a tale."

At that moment there was a fanfare of trumpets, the door at the end of the hall flew open and, preceded by two officers in full dress uniform, Prince Carl strode in with stately step. The assemblage bowed low, with the exception of Rance Cameron and, Rance noted with surprise, Mary Stewart. She caught his glance and whispered:

"*I* am no longer a member of a buffoon court. I, like yourself, am an American!"

Cameron shook his head, wondering vaguely how many more surprises were hidden in this small and most surprising person.

Again to Cameron's surprise, the meal that followed was not dulled by a stodgy atmosphere. Once seated, with a mug at his elbow and a full plate before him, Prince Carl relaxed his dignity and proved to be a pleasant and entertaining host. Mary sat on his left, Count Otto on his right. Cameron was seated next to Mary.

The prince asked many questions relative to

the country, its people and conditions, and the questions were shrewd and pointed. Count Otto's interest in rangeland problems was unexpected; he inquired about the possibilities for farming and irrigation, the improvement of cattle through breeding and similar matters. His English was stumbling, but he managed to make himself understood. Prince Carl, undoubtedly an expert linguist, would from time to time translate Cameron's answers. Cameron experienced a growing respect for the young nobleman.

"We have learned much," Prince Carl said as the dinner drew to a close. "*Herr* Cameron, we find ourselves deeper and deeper in your debt. You are a difficult person with whom to associate," he added whimsically. "One feels weighed down by a sense of obligation."

"What little I have to offer is small indeed when compared with what you are doing for the country and your people," Cameron replied.

The prince smiled at the answer and nodded his head with approbation. "Maria, we will make a courtier of him yet," he said. "He is made for it. He has the turn of thought and the trick of speech."

Mary Stewart smiled and did not reply.

It was late when the dinner finally ended. Prince Carl soon departed for his quarters.

"I have much to do," he told Cameron. "Far into the night I must labor, for all is not frivolity here. I hope you will pardon my little foibles; they relax me for the many problems that confront me."

A little later Cameron said good night to Mary and Count Otto and repaired to his own room. He drew a chair to the window and sat gazing gloomily at the starlit rangeland. He grudgingly wondered how any woman could resist the vivacious young nobleman; it seemed that Count Otto indeed had everything. A range tramp in overalls was something of a contrast, and an unenviable contrast. He rolled and lighted a cigarette and stared at the stars without seeing them.

Three uneventful days followed. Cameron got to know a good many of the people of the fort, and liked them. Most were irresponsible, even frivolous, but others were grave men and women with a philosophy of life with which he could find no fault. He quickly learned that these last were political refugees who had been banished on account of strong opinions that did not coincide with those held by the rulers of the land. Here they were utterly out of their element, but nevertheless resolved to start a new life where they would not undergo oppression. Cameron formed a high opinion of them.

He saw little of Mary Stewart during the three days. She was often in the company of Count Otto, and Cameron admitted he couldn't blame her; Count Otto was certainly likable, despite his waywardness and his fondness for drink, gambling and women.

In the course of a conversation with Count Otto, Cameron surprised depths in the young man's nature he would not have believed existed. The talk had turned to social and political conditions in Germany. Count Otto spoke of them in his halting English with a flushed face and flashing eyes.

"Ach! it is horrible," he declared. "Our rulers fritter away the wealth of the land in perverted pleasures. They are selfish, cruel, greedy. They look upon the peasants as dirt under their feet. They are arrogant, contemptuous of the rights of men, thinking of nothing but their own pleasures and well-being. They persecute the Jews. Why should the Jews be persecuted? They are people just as you and I. They feel, they suffer, they love, they show compassion toward their fellow men. They have their joys and their sorrows just as you and I, their hope and ambitions. Why should they be persecuted because they do not see eye to eye with others in religious matters? Who knows for sure what is the true faith? They may be wrong, or we may be wrong, who knows? And really it does not greatly matter which is right and which is wrong. There is one end to all, and as our lives are lived that end will be. Persecution! It is a horrible word! Why should anybody be persecuted? Your *Herr* Rosenthal, whom we know and respect—why should anyone want to persecute him because of a difference in viewpoint relative to religious matters? It is injustice, and as sure as there is a God in Heaven, that injustice will be punished. *Ach!* Germany will some day pay for injustice in blood and tears!" He paused, and his winning smile flashed out.

"*Herr* Cameron, I am young, but I think," he said. "I was born to great wealth, but is that wealth mine? No! I am but the trustee for those who come after me, and if I fail in my trusteeship, I shall regret. Ha! I will take me to the flowing bowl and my sorrows drown!"

Cameron experienced a heightened respect for the vivacious young nobleman, and a corresponding depression of his own spirits. He definitely resolved to leave New Braunfels on the morrow. He should have done it three days before, he told himself morosely. There was certainly nothing to be gained from staying any longer. Like Count Otto, he felt an inclination to drown his sorrows in the flowing bowl, but tonight he didn't. He repaired to his room, rolled a cigarette and once again sat trying to stare the unsympathetic stars out of countenance.

CHAPTER VIII

The next morning Cameron was lying between waking and sleeping, drowsily thinking over the events of the night before, when Henry tapped on the door.

"Thought maybe you'd like to give our little settlement the once-over," the young officer explained.

Cameron agreed it wasn't a bad notion; and after breakfast, which he shared with Henry in a small room off the kitchen, the rest of the fort's occupants apparently being still asleep, the horses were brought around and they set out on their tour of inspection.

Cameron liked what he saw. The small houses were well built and with plenty of land. Every-thing was orderly and spotlessly clean, the peo-

ple busy and cheerful. His estimate of Prince
Carl's ability rose. If only the man would recon-
cile himself to remaining here and supervise and
encourage his project instead of chasing off after
moonbeams, Cameron felt the community would
prosper and grow.

"I want you to see our river," Henry said. "I
firmly believe it's the shortest one in the land
carrying a large volume of water. It rises at
Comal Springs and empties into the Guadalupe.
We call it Comal River. It's only four miles
long and all within the town's limits as laid out."

A little later they reached the stream, which
Cameron thought was all Henry claimed it to be.
Deep, clear and full-running, it wound through
the settlement. Along its banks was a luxuriant
growth of giant caladiums, whose broad, shield-
like leaves added a tropical note to the scenery.

"Plenty of water power here for mills and
such," Cameron commented. "All you need are
a few dams."

"That will come in time, I trust," Henry replied. "This should be a fine town some day."

After returning to the fort, Cameron hunted
up Bert, whom he found looking somewhat the
worse for wear.

"A real nice place, this," Bert declared. "My head feels big as a barrel. These folks drink something they claim is beer, but it's got more wallop than redeye. I ain't going to let it whup me, though; got a date with the wranglers and the kitchen help for another session tonight. How you doing?"

"Okay," Cameron replied.

"Going to stick around here awhile?"

"I guess so," Cameron admitted. "Haven't gotten any orders yet concerning the wagon."

Bert glanced at him sideways and appeared to be stifling a grin. "Had a notion you would," he said. "Papa Rosenthal said he felt sure you would."

"The devil he did!"

"Uh-huh," nodded Bert. "He seemed to find something funny about it; he chuckled a lot while he was telling me. He told me to stick around, too, till I got word from him. Wonder what he saw that was so funny?"

Cameron regarded the teamster suspiciously. He had a feeling that Bert also "saw something funny." Bert looked too darned innocent to be true.

Late that afternon the wagon train from Carlshafen arrived. Prince Carl was on hand to greet it, and so was Rance Cameron. He was surprised to see Lije Fitch riding at the head of the guards.

Fitch was evidently also surprised to see him. He glowered and muttered something under his breath.

"Thought you'd be riding west by now," he said harshly.

"You shouldn't think so much, Lije," Cameron countered; "you'll lame your brain."

"Might have been a good notion if you had," Fitch said, adding significantly, "The climate hereabouts has been known to be unhealthy for some folks."

"Yes, you're right," Cameron agreed. "It was that way for several gents just a few nights back. By the way, I don't seem to see one of your guards, a little scrawny jigger with a broken nose and a scar on his chin."

Fitch's jaw sagged, and for an instant he looked decidedly startled.

"What the devil you talking about?" he demanded. "I ain't never had nobody like that working for me."

"No?" Cameron said. "Funny, I could have sworn he was one of your guards. Must have been some other train, or maybe *he* found the climate unhealthy."

He turned and walked away. Fitch glared after him, his mouth working.

A little later Cameron spoke to Bert. "That little hellion with the broken nose we left down in the clearing was one of Fitch's hands," he told the teamster. "I described him to Fitch and scared the stuffing out of him."

"You didn't tell him where you saw the guy?"

"No," Cameron answered. "I figured it best to let him puzzle his head over it and worry a bit."

"Maybe you were right," Bert conceded, "but keep your eyes skun. Fitch is bad, and he ain't forgetting what you did to him in the Best Chance."

"I doubt if he'll carry it any farther," Cameron predicted.

"Maybe not," said Bert, plainly unconvinced, "but look out for a knife in your back. I wouldn't put anything past the devil." He strode off to speak with a teamster he knew. Cameron felt a touch on his elbow and turned to face Mary Stewart. Her eyes looked even wider than usual and seemed filled with dark shadows.

"What did he mean by that last remark?" she demanded peremptorily.

"Oh, Bert's always imagining something," Cameron replied.

"He never struck me as being an imaginative person. I gathered from what he said that you are in danger."

"Nothing to worry about," he deprecated.

"I'm not so sure," she differed. "Come on up to the fort now, and you're staying there tonight if I have to tie you. Come along; the prince wants to see you."

"And very likely the count wants to see you," he remarked teasingly.

"If he does he's not afraid to look for me," she retorted. "Come along. I don't feel safe about you being down here."

"Mary," he asked, "would you care if something happened to me?"

"Yes, you know I would!" she answered. "Now shut up and come along."

CHAPTER IX

When they arrived at the fort, an officer immediately led Cameron to the prince's presence. He found the colonizer seated behind a massive table desk covered with maps and papers. He waved Cameron to a chair and for a while sat fingering some documents and apparently thinking deeply. Finally he raised his eyes.

"*Herr* Cameron," he said, "I believe I am safe in assuming that you have no personal interest in this community, its aims and its ambitions?"

"Yes, I think you are safe in assuming so," Cameron replied. "In fact, I was but vaguely aware of it until a short time ago."

The prince nodded and for a moment sat gazing out the window. When he resumed the conversation he spoke slowly, evidently choosing his words with care.

"This project was launched by an association of German noblemen known as the Society for the Protection of German Immigrants in Texas," he explained, "which association has undertaken to place a large number of colonists. Of this association I am the head, at least the nominal head. There has been considerable difference of opinion among the members, and some of my policies and methods have been criticized, particularly by the man who will quite likely in time succeed me here, Baron Hans von Meusebach. Of course they have every right to criticize constructively, which is fundamental to a democratic body such as the association. Much of the criticism had been directed at my appointment of the man who represents me at Carlshafen and directs operations there, *Herr* Mark Sterns." The stubborn chin jutted forward. "I have every faith in *Herr* Sterns and greatly desire to see him vindicated of the charges that have been leveled at him by Baron von Meusebach and others. I believe a thorough and unprejudiced investigation of *Herr* Sterns' activities *will* vindicate him. I am requesting you to conduct that investigation and report your findings to me. I will greatly appreciate it if you will agree to do so, and your remuneration will be adequate."

Cameron regarded him for a moment before replying, turning over in his mind the surprising and unlooked for proposition.

"But do you consider, sir, that I am qualified to conduct such an investigation?" he asked.

"I do," replied the prince. "We agree that you have no personal interest in the project and so would not be motivated in any way by self-interest. You would approach it with an open mind and, I am convinced, would report the truth as you recognized it. And that is just what I desire. I will repeat, I have great confidence in *Herr* Sterns, but if it is proven by your findings that my confidence is misplaced, I will act accordingly."

Again Cameron sat for some moments in thought. "But what methods am I supposed to utilize in such an investigation?" he asked.

"That," smiled the prince, "I leave to your native intelligence. Your methods will be your own and I will not interfere in any way."

Apparently sensing that Cameron was mulling over the proposition, he continued, the dreaminess of his eyes intensified.

"I do not expect to be here much longer," he stated. "I have many projects in view in other lands."

Here he goes, Cameron thought, chasing after moonbeams.

"My country is overpopulated and steadily becoming more so," the prince resumed. "We must find an outlet for our surplus. Most of those who are leaving now are fleeing political reprisals, but many more will leave, seeking homes and a chance to grow. I must provide them with opportunity to expand. But before I leave here, I greatly desire that all controversial matters be cleared up. So what do you say, *Herr* Cameron?"

"Well, sir," Cameron smiled, "I greatly appreciate your confidence in my ability, although I am not at all sure that confidence will be justified. I am out of work at the moment, so I'll take the job and do the best I can for you."

"And I am confident that your best will be ample," the prince instantly returned. He opened a drawer and drew forth a small canvas bag that clinked.

"For necessary expenses," he said. "But do not

rush away from New Braunfels," he added. "Rest up for a few days from your recent harrowing experience. We will do the best we can to make your sojourn pleasant." He rose to his feet to signify that the interview was at an end. Cameron slipped the bag of gold pieces into his pocket, thanked Prince Carl and took his departure, his mind in something of a whirl.

He was honest enough with himself to admit that he had accepted the unusual commission because it would give him an excuse and opportunity for keeping in touch with New Braunfels, and again experienced an uneasy conviction that he would be making a fool of himself by so doing. Well, he couldn't help it, and Mary's impulsive remark down in the village and her expressed concern for his safety had opened a tiny avenue of hope. Anyhow, he was committed and would have to go through with the business.

He wondered as to the reasons for the prince's act and, considering the matter, decided that quite likely Johan had had a hand in the business. Viewed in this light, the affair appeared less preposterous. Prince Carl, despite his idiosyncrasies, was anything but a fool. He would realize that he, Cameron, was the last person anybody in Carlshafen would suspect of being his emissary. Cameron might be able to learn things that would be carefully concealed from anyone known to represent the prince.

Well, he was in for it and would have to go through with it. He recalled that both John Rafferty, the Best Chance owner, and Papa Rosenthal had a poor opinion of Mark Sterns, and they were both men of mature judgment. Perhaps the critical members of the Society were right and Sterns was mixed up in something off-color. The fact that he had hired Lije Fitch's wagons to transport the newly arrived batch of colonists did not tend to raise him in Cameron's estimation. Just how he was to go about getting the lowdown on Sterns' activities he had not the least notion at the moment, but circumstances might offer the opportunity. He'd do the best he could.

Reaching the main hall of the fort, still pondering the assignment, he mingled with members of the prince's little personal retinue. And again he sensed the pathetic melancholy hidden beneath a cloak of false gaiety. These poor people were not happy. They were totally out of touch with their surroundings and would never be able to adapt themselves to the environment into which they had been projected. Henry was right: they wouldn't last long here. When the prince moved on, as inevitably he would, they also would depart, to follow him to new adventures or to return to the homeland for which they longed. In the village below the citadel, roots were being sent down, roots that would draw welcome sustenance from the land, but not here. To these people the soil was parched and unprofitable. If they remained, there would be a steady withering away to extinction.

Some time later Mary Stewart appeared. As she approached him her lips were compressed, her eyes distinctly stormy. Cameron wondered if he had offended her in some way. His mind was quickly set at ease on that score, however.

"I just had an interview with my uncle," she announced. "He suggested it was time I was thinking of marrying Count Otto; I said it wasn't. He said that it was his desire that I marry the count without delay; I said no. He insisted that I change my mind; I said I wouldn't. He grew definitely angry and flatly ordered me to obey him and marry Otto at once. I just as flatly told him that this was America, where women take orders from no man. There were strong words. I think had this been Almain, he would have clapped me in a dungeon."

"But why did you refuse to marry the Count?" Cameron asked half jestingly. Immediately his suspicion that Mary Stewart had a temper was confirmed.

"I don't believe you care a jot whether I marry him or not!" she blazed, and stormed away. Cameron gazed after her, shaking his head.

She didn't appear at dinner. Nor, for that matter, did Count Otto. Cameron wondered uncomfortably if they might be together, which thought did not improve his appetite. After the meal was finished and Prince Carl, in anything but a good temper, had departed to his study, Cameron joined a group of roisterers at the far end of the long table. He soon agreed with Bert, the teamster, that what these folks drank was potent and realized he'd do better to take it a bit easy, but failed to do so. He was beginning to be imbued with a growing spirit of recklessness; his thoughts turned to the town below the fort. Lije Fitch would be there, very likely getting drunk in one of the few taverns. Why not go down and have it out with the hellion once and for all? The more he drank the more alluring the notion seemed. It was pleasant here, and he had plenty of not unattractive feminine companionship, apparently not in the least affected by the contrast his rangeland garb afforded with the silken clothes of the courtiers, but he'd like to have a showdown with Fitch. He vaguely conceded that it was a feeling similar to that which had seethed within his being when he stalked the McPhersons of Calvert Valley.

This is what you came a thousand miles to get away from, some watchful monitor in his brain reminded him; but the warning was unheeded. He slipped away from the group and headed for his own room and his guns.

When he opened the door he got an unexpected and not unpleasant surprise. Seated in a chair by the window was Mary Stewart. She regarded him coolly.

"Well, get through flirting with the *frauleins*?" she asked.

"I chiefly flirted with a glass," he replied. "Why didn't you come to dinner?"

"Because I didn't want to."

"I noticed Count Otto wasn't there, either."

"And if you'd looked, and known whom to

look for, you'd have noticed that the Baroness Houthem wasn't there, either. Otto is true to all women, when he is with them. How did you make out with the prince this afternoon? Tell me about it."

He told her everything, omitting no details. She did not appear particularly surprised, and Cameron abruptly saw a hand other than Johan's in the business.

"Mary, why did you do it?" he asked.

"Because I wanted to," she replied. Without giving him time to comment, she continued, "Besides, I really believe you may be able to do the prince some good. He's stubborn to the verge of stupidity when his judgment is questioned, but he can be prevailed upon to change his mind if shown conclusively that he is wrong. I am more concerned, however, about the people who will soon be pouring into the country. I know that *Herr* Rosenthal, who was my father's friend in his youth, does not trust that man Mark Sterns. It occurred to me that, aside from other and perhaps more personal desires, you could be of service to those who will greatly need help. I'm not worried about my uncle; he'll make out no matter what happens. He is painfully capable of taking care of himself."

"Do you dislike him?" Cameron asked curiously.

"No, I don't," she replied, "and I don't think he dislikes me, although at times I think he resents me because he loved my mother. He named this place Sophienberg in honor of her memory. And the Prince of Auerswald, his half-brother, won her."

"I think I can understand that," Cameron said slowly.

She smiled a little and changed the subject. "I suppose you're wondering why I came here," she said. "Well, I figured you'd hardly go down below tonight without your guns, so I came here to keep a watch on them and make sure you didn't get them. I really believe you had a notion to go down there, looking for trouble."

Cameron flushed a little and did not answer.

"Well, you're not going," she said flatly. "Not if I can keep you here, and I think I can. She rose as she spoke and looked him squarely in the eyes.

"Yes," he agreed soberly. "I believe you can."

"And perhaps," she added, "by now you can believe that if anything happened to you, it would mean for me a great and lasting sorrow?"

"That's what I want to believe," he answered thickly.

"Believe it!" she said. "And I have your word you won't go to the lower town tonight?"

"Yes," he replied, "you have it."

"That's enough," she said. "Good night, Rance."

"Good night, Mary."

She stood on tiptoe, kissed him lightly on the lips and was gone. Rance Cameron walked to the window and stood gazing at the star-strewn heavens. In his heart was peace and a quiet happiness.

CHAPTER X

From the window they watched the wagon train depart from the settlement below.

"I'm glad to see them go," Mary said, "and I don't want you to leave here soon enough to catch up with them on the road."

"They're not heading directly for Carlshafen," Cameron answered. "Bert told me that they plan to turn off to San Antonio, about twenty-five miles from here, and pick up loads. They'll likely be in San Antonio several days."

"That's better," she said. "Now I won't be so bothered when you leave for Carlshafen."

That afternoon a horseman was observed climbing the slope to the fort.

"Why, it's Cliff Hardy, Jim Rivercomb's range boss!" exclaimed Bert, who was standing in front of the fort talking with Cameron.

A few minutes later the grizzled old Walking R foreman pulled to a halt beside them and swung down from the hull.

"Howdy," he said. "I was looking for you, Rance."

Cameron spoke a word to Henry, who was present, and a wrangler was called to take care of Hardy's mount.

"What's on your mind, Cliff?" Cameron asked.

"Jim and Papa Rosenthal sent me here with a word for you," the range boss replied. "They want you back in Indianola—that's what everybody's took to calling that darn town—as soon as you can get there."

"How'd they know I'd be here?" Cameron replied. "I told them I was heading west."

"They seemed to figure otherwise, and laughed together a little about it," Hardy answered. "They—" He broke off and gazed in frank admiration at something behind Cameron, who felt a touch on his elbow. He turned to face Mary.

"Reckon I understand now how they knew you'd be here," Hardy remarked.

"This gentleman is one of experience," Mary observed.

"That's right, ma'am," nodded the range boss. "These young squirts think they know a lot, but they're terrapin-brained, because they haven't lived long enough to learn anything."

Mary laughed and held out her slender hand. "You must be one of Rance's friends, so of course you're mine," she said.

Hardy bared his grizzled head and bowed over the hand.

"Guess that goes both ways, ma'am," he said.

"Come on in," the girl invited. "I imagine you want something to eat after your long ride."

"Well, I could stand a surroundin' about now," Hardy admitted.

Henry led the way to the little dining room in which he and Cameron ate together and made sure all of Hardy's wants were adequately provided for.

"And now, Cliff, what's on your mind?" Cameron asked when they were alone.

"Nothing much more than what I've already told you. Papa and Jim want to see you. I think it's something to do with the Dutchies who are piling into town—three shiploads in the past week—where Papa's concerned. Jim wants to talk to you about something else. I'm pulling out, Rance, in a couple of months or so."

"You're pulling out!"

"Yep. I bought the Hogadorn spread over to the west of the Walking R and aim to set up in business for myself. About time, I figure. And I think Jim wants you for range boss after I'm gone. I know he had it in mind before you decided to leave.

"And the range boss lives in a little house by himself, and of course the house will be there after I leave," he added meaningly. "Mom and me won't need it any more."

"What makes you think I'll need it?" Cameron asked.

"She'll tell you what you need and don't need," Hardy replied. "I know; I ain't been married for forty years without learning something. She's sure a purty gal and looks nice. You're lucky."

After finishing his meal, Hardy went off somewhere with Bert, probably to share a potation or two with the wranglers and kitchen help. Cameron obtained an interview with Prince Carl and explained the message he had received.

"Good!" exclaimed the prince. "It should work in admirably with our plans and further them. It will give you reason for being at Carlshafen and for visiting New Braunfels, which you will unquestionably be glad to do. I. am sorry to see certain cherished plans of mine go to naught, but a man is foolish to found his hopes on the variable whims of a woman." His winning smile transformed his face.

"I wish you all happiness, my son. Take an old man's blessing."

Cameron bowed his head. "Thank you, sir," he said. "I promise that you will never have cause to regret this."

"I'm confident I will not," said the prince. His face grew sad. "Happy indeed is the man who gains the love of the woman he loves," he added. "I have never known it. Well, life brings many a cross; who is without them? May you prosper, my son, and forget not those who need."

Cameron left his presence feeling a trifle sad himself. The simple confession bursting from the old man's lonely heart affected him deeply.

He told Mary of his conversation with the prince. "He certainly didn't appear particularly displeased with us," he concluded.

"Oh, he's all right," she replied. "He hates to be crossed in anything, is unpredictable, and flies off the handle quickly, but he's easily appeased. He never was a selfish autocrat in anything. He just labors under the illusion that Papa always knows best."

Cameron chuckled. "And I suppose the count will be broken-hearted," he observed.

"Not at all," she said. "On the contrary, I think he'll feel relieved. He prefers the baroness, among others, and only agreed to go along with the marriage because the prince told him to. Really, I think he has the horror of marriage that afflicts any philanderer. He would always be put to the trouble of thinking up alibis and excuses, and he doesn't like to have to think. Don't worry about Otto; he'll go dancing on, continually getting singed but always coming back for more."

Cameron laughed aloud, and turned the conversation to more serious matters.

"I'll have to be leaving in the morning," he said.

Her eyes clouded. "You'll be careful, dear, won't you?" she said. "Please be, for now you have something to live for, or at least I hope you feel you have."

"I'm not liable to forget it," he answered. He

proceeded to tell her what Hardy said about Jim Rivercomb's intentions and the little house the range boss occupied. She listened, wide-eyed.

"That will be perfect," she declared. "We don't have a thing to worry about, once you've finished the business for the prince."

Cameron and Cliff Hardy rode away from New Braunfels the following morning; Bert would follow later with the wagon. As he went to get Smoke from the stable, Bert accompanied him.

"I did some things to your hull last night," he announced. "I made a saddle boot and fastened it on and shoved old Bellerin' Betsy in it. Them Colts of yours are all right, but they won't carry a big hunk of lead a mile like that old cannon. Don't worry about me. Johan gave me a brace of pistols, good ones; and besides, nobody is apt to bother an empty wagon."

"What makes you think I might need it?" Cameron asked, glancing at the big Sharps snugged in the leather sheath.

Bert shrugged his shoulders. "Never can tell in this section," he replied. "And yesterday some gents rode away from here who sure ain't head over heels in love with you. They might figure out something correctly."

Cameron nodded. There was truth in what Bert said. "Thanks a lot," he said. "I hope I won't have any use for it, but it could come in handy. A jigger a half-mile away isn't safe from a Sharps."

At the bottom of the slope, Cameron glanced back at the little figure standing in front of the fort. He waved his hand and then faced resolutely to the front. For the first time in many years he wasn't getting any pleasure from riding away from a place.

On their good horses they made excellent progress, and night found them well beyond the point where the trail branched to reach San Antonio. As they passed the fork, neither saw the rider sitting his horse in the shelter of a thicket, from which he had a view of the main trail. He watched them ride out of sight, then turned his mount and rode swiftly toward San Antonio.

Cameron and Hardy made camp that night on the bank of a little stream. They cooked a simple but appetizing meal from the provisions they carried in their saddle pouches and rode on with the dawn, entering the loneliest and most forbidding stretch they would have to pass over on their way to the coast.

Toward evening, from the crest of a rise, Cameron glanced back and saw seven horsemen about half a mile distant riding swiftly in their direction. He studied them a moment, then spoke to Hardy. The old range boss eyed the approaching group, his brow puckering.

"Wonder what they're doing out here?" he said. "Rance, I'm beginning to get a notion. Speed up a bit, now, and let's see what happens."

They rode on at a faster pace. Glancing back a little later, they saw the seven had also speeded up and were quite a bit closer.

"Son," Hardy said, "I believe they're after us and they mean business. Bert had the right notion. I met Lije Fitch and his bunch on the trail yesterday, and they sure gave me a close once-over. Reckon they figured I was headed for New Braunfels to see you and that you'd be riding back with me. I'd bet a hatful of pesos they had a hellion posted at the San Antonio fork yesterday to keep a lookout for us. Yes, sir, I'll bet that's it. Ride, son; we've got trouble on our hands."

They rode, at the fastest pace Hardy could get out of his big roan, but it wasn't quite enough;

the pursuit gained slowly but steadily. Cameron knew that if he gave Smoke his head he'd soon outdistance the group, but Hardy's horse wasn't Smoke. He glanced back, estimated the distance. "About four hundred yards," he muttered. "I should be able to do something at that range." He drew the Sharps from the saddle boot. "Hold it, Smoke!" he called.

Instantly the great moros plunged to a halt. Cameron whirled him, raised the rifle to his shoulder and glanced along the sights. Getting a fine bead on the foremost horseman, he squeezed the stock. The Sharps boomed, gushing a cloud of smoke. The pursuing rider threw up his hands, reeled sideways and fell. His horse stumbled, and for a moment the others were thrown into confusion.

"Ride!" Cameron shouted to Hardy, who had also pulled up. He whirled Smoke again and sent him charging after the roan.

Loading the big rifle on horseback was a chore, but Cameron finally managed it, at the price of precious distance lost. When he glanced back again, the pursuers had cut the four hundred yards to less than three. He twisted in the saddle and tried another shot with the Sharps.

He saw a man reel slightly but keep his seat by leaning forward and clinging to the saddle horn. He thrust the rifle into the boot and turned to the front; there was no chance to reload again.

The pursuers came on, but now they held their distance. Cameron quickly divined what they had in mind. Night was not far off, and soon it would be too dark for him accurately to aim the rifle. Then they would close in for the kill, with the advantage of numbers all theirs.

"Looks bad," he called to Hardy, "but maybe we can give those devils a surprise. There's a big bend in the trail ahead, around a hill, and we'll be out of sight for a while."

"Figure to ride into the brush?" Hardy called back.

"Wouldn't work," Cameron replied. "They'd hunt us down. No, I've got a better idea. Get everything you can out of your horse."

The trail began bending around the hill, and they lost sight of the pursuit. Cameron estimated the distance they covered on the curving track.

"All right," he said. "Pull up and back into the edge of the brush."

Hardy did as he was told. Together they sat their blowing mounts, watching the sharp angle of the trail behind, where it jutted around a bulge of cliff. Cameron drew his Colt, made sure that the second gun under his belt on the left side was easily accessible.

"Now if they'll just fall for it," he muttered.

Hardy had a brace of big horse pistols. He drew and cocked them. "Steady, son," he said, "and don't get any highfalutin notions of fair play. It's them or us. Let 'em have it soon as they show."

"Don't worry, I've been through this sort of thing before," Cameron returned.

"Shoot fast and shoot straight or you won't be through it again," Hardy said grimly. "Get set; I hear 'em."

Around the bend bulged the pursuers, one swaying in his saddle. Cameron and Hardy instantly opened fire. Cameron pulled trigger as fast as he could cock the Colt, slammed it empty into its holster and drew the second gun. Hardy's pistols boomed.

The blazing volley emptied two saddles. Cameron began firing with his second Colt as the pursuers pulled up in wild confusion; another man fell. The remaining three, with yells and curses, wheeled their horses and rode madly back the way they had come. The drumming of the hoofs swiftly faded into the distance.

"Got a bellyful, eh?" old Cliff growled. "We won't see any more of *them,* son. Let's take a look at what we bagged."

Dismounting, they examined the three dead men lying sprawled in the dust.

"I don't recall seeing any of them with Fitch's wagons," Cameron said.

"Me neither," replied Hardy. "Didn't expect to. Fitch would be too smart to use his own hands for such a chore. You can hire all the gunmen you want in San Antonio for a few pesos."

The three riderless horses had run into the brush a little way and stopped. Cameron got the rigs off them and turned them loose, knowing they would fend for themselves till somebody picked them up.

"Let's go," said Hardy. "When Fitch comes along and sees this buzzard bait in the trail, maybe it'll give him a bit of a jolt. He'll hear about it from the three who got away, of course, but seeing 'em is different from hearing about 'em."

"I'm a bit worried about Bert," Cameron said. "I don't want him to run into trouble."

"They won't bother with him," Hardy returned. "To Fitch's way of thinking, he ain't nobody. Besides, he didn't figure to start out till today. Chances are he'll be behind them. He'll get through, all right."

Cameron still had some misgivings as to the teamster's safety, but he let the older man's counsel prevail. They rode on, continuing until well after dark and making a fireless camp. They made good time the next day and reached Victoria a couple of hours before sunset. They no longer feared pursuit and spent a comfortable night in the town. With no further mishap, they reached Carlshafen the following evening.

CHAPTER XI

As they rode into the settlement, Cameron saw a number of tents and shacks hastily thrown together with raw lumber dotting the prairie. Hardy frowned at them.

"That's where the Dutchies are squattin'," he remarked with a shake of his head. I'm scared they're in for trouble if they don't get out of here soon. That's no way to live in this climate. They're asking for cholera or Yellow Jack. What the devil's the matter with Mark Sterns? He knew they were coming, so why didn't he make provisions for them?"

Cameron shook his own head, and they rode on. He was very much of the opinion that Papa Rosenthal and the Baron von Meusebach had the right notion in distrusting Mark Sterns. He resolved to get in touch with Rosenthal without delay.

First, however, he stopped at the Best Chance for something to eat and a chat with John Rafferty.

The saloonkeeper greeted him with a warm hand clasp and a chuckle. "Back even sooner than I expected," he said. "Well, was I right?"

"John, you were," Cameron conceded. "She's the grandest girl in the world."

"Thought she was okay when I saw her that first day snuggled in your arms up top of Smoke," Rafferty chuckled. "She looked like that was right where she belonged, and I figured she'd work out a way to stay there."

"I guess she did," Cameron smiled.

"Understand she's a real princess," said Rafferty.

"She was, but now she's a Texas girl," Cameron replied.

"And you're a Texas man?"

"John," Cameron admitted, "for the first time since I landed here, I'm beginning to believe I am."

Hardy, who had paused outside to speak with an acquaintance, came in, and they ate together.

Afterwards Cameron headed for Papa Rosenthal's house, where he was greeted with effusive warmth.

"Tell me about everything that happened," said Rosenthal.

Cameron told him. Papa clucked over the fight in the clearing. "I feared something of the kind might occur," he said. "That is why I wished you to accompany the wagon. The gold did not matter so much, but I was anxious for the welfare of Her—Miss Stewart. How did you get along with her?"

Cameron grinned. "So well that I reckon I'm slated to be getting along with her the rest of my life," he admitted.

Papa Rosenthal chuckled delightedly. "I expected as much," he said. "Times before have I seen a woman regard a man as she did you. I am not at all surprised, and I am very pleased. I knew she could not be other than a fine girl. Her father and her mother were wonderful people. I knew them both well. I was paired with the prince, her father, in the *schlager* fights at the University, the mock duels with the broadsword, considered friendly tests of courage and skill, but the scars of which were often carried by the combatants to their graves. After I came to America I corresponded with the prince and her mother, and after they passed on, with the daughter. That is why she came at once to me when she arrived here."

He paused a moment, looking thoughtful.

"Both parents died when the girl was very young," he resumed. "It was her mother's last request that Maria be reared and educated in Scotland and England, and Prince Carl, who was Maria's guardian, respected the dead woman's wish. Not until Maria reached her majority did he summon her back to Germany, for the purpose of contracting a marriage with Count Otto, I gather. Strange, isn't it, that the dying mother should express such a desire. Perhaps she foresaw a day when a knowledge of the English tongue and familiarity with the customs and ways of thinking of Scotland, a free land, would work to her daughter's advantage; who can tell? It did appear to work out that way. But go on with your story; I would hear more."

Rosenthal was greatly interested in the mission Cameron had contracted to perform for the prince.

"I've a notion Solms-Braunfels is himself beginning to wonder a bit about Sterns," he said. "Well, he'll find he has plenty to wonder about. The way Sterns has handled the situation here is downright criminal. The immigrants are pouring in, and he has made no adequate provisions for their proper care. Everybody knew what was going to happen, and he took no precautions against what will inevitably take place. Word has come that the convention at Austin has approved the annexation resolution already passed by both houses of Congress, and Texas is virtually a state in the union. The ratification of the state constitution, the approval of Congress and the vote of admittance are only formalities. Mexico has threatened that it would regard the annexation of Texas as a declaration of war by the United States. There's going to be a war, all right. The Federal Government is already sending troops. There will be no adequate transportation available for the colonists. The contracts the teamsters have made with Sterns are going to be broken, for with war in the offing, they'll be able to get much higher-paying contracts. In fact, that's already started. Sterns must have realized what was going to happen months ago, but he made no move to prepare against it."

"I wonder why the devil he didn't buy wagons and hire drivers?" Cameron remarked. "I understand there is plenty of money behind the project."

"Plenty," agreed Rosenthal. "Money is one thing Solms-Braunfels does not lack. What he does lack is judgment in choosing those who spend it for him. Sterns hasn't bought wagons and has not even contracted for them. At this late date he'll have trouble getting them in time, if he tries, which he has shown no indication of doing."

"Do you think he's feathering his own nest with the money he handles for the prince?" Cameron asked.

"If he is, it is going to be very difficult to prove anything against him," Rosenthal replied gloomily. "He's shrewd, very shrewd, and far-sighted, and will be adept at covering his tracks. Getting something on him is going to be considerable of a chore."

"Well, that's the chore Prince Carl handed me." Cameron smiled. "Sort of in reverse, of course. He is anxious to see Sterns vindicated where mistakes or wrongdoing are concerned, or so he said. That's what I'm supposed to do. But he gave me a free hand, and if I show Sterns up as a hairpin, he'll still feel he got his money's worth."

"If you manage to dig up the truth, I predict he'll get a good deal more than his money's worth," Rosenthal snorted. "But it won't be easy; Sterns is crafty."

"I've noticed that his sort usually slips somehow, sooner or later."

"Maybe." Rosenthal was plainly dubious. "Of one thing I'm convinced: he's got Lije Fitch working with him."

"And there is where he may have made his slip," Cameron said slowly. "I believe Fitch is vulnerable, and if he's roped he'll very likely drag Sterns down with him. I consider him capable of just that."

"I wonder why Sterns took up with a man like Fitch?" Rosenthal commented.

"Perhaps he couldn't help it," Cameron suggested. "Maybe Fitch managed somehow to get something on him, and Sterns has to play along. That's not beyond the realm of possibility, I'd say."

"You could be right," Rosenthal agreed. "It's worth thinking about, anyhow."

"Getting back to the immigrants, what are we going to do about them?" Cameron asked.

"I don't know," Rosenthal admitted. "The prime necessity is to get them out of Indianola as quickly as possible. I've placed all my wagons at their disposal, but as you know, I have only a few. I hope to get a train moving without delay."

A little later, when Cameron stood up to go, Rosenthal said, "Drop in at the store in the morning. Jim Rivercomb is going to be there and wants to talk to you."

Cameron promised and rode back to town. He paused at the Best Chance for a drink with Rafferty, and told the saloonkeeper what Rosenthal had to say about the transportation problem.

"And he's going to use his wagons, eh?" Rafferty commented. "I've a notion Sterns won't like it."

"He'll have to like it," Cameron replied.

"Uh-huh, but Papa may be in for trouble with him," said Rafferty. "He's a mean sort of cuss, or I make a mistake, and he's got Lije Fitch with him. Sort of a bad combination to go up against, Rance. Sterns has the brains and Fitch has the men."

"We'll chance it," Cameron replied. "I think

we can handle them."

"Papa Rosenthal ain't no zero," Rafferty nodded. "I reckon he'll be able to hold his own, with you lending a hand. Let's have another drink."

Cameron dropped into Rosenthal's store fairly early the next morning. He found Papa alone in his office in the back of the store, busy with some correspondence. He nodded to a chair and went on writing. After a bit, he laid his pen aside and regarded Cameron with his twinkling eyes.

"Jim hasn't shown up yet, but I reckon he'll be along soon," he remarked. "Nice fellow, Rivercomb."

"I've always found him okay," Cameron agreed. "Smart cowman, too; none better."

Papa nodded and glanced out the window "Here comes Mark Sterns," he said. "Reckon maybe he's got a thing or two to say to me."

Cameron stood up and glanced around. A door from the office led into another back room that was used for storage. "I want to hear what he has to say, but I'd rather he didn't see me until after he's said it," he announced. "I'm going to slip into the back room for a while."

Rosenthal nodded, and Cameron walked into the other room. It was unlighted, and from where he stood he could see and not be seen. A moment later he heard Sterns' step, and the agent entered the office.

Mark Sterns was sallow, tall and spare and clean-shaven, with a hooked nose and bright eyes—the face of an able and adroit man. Mark Sterns was both. Cameron understood that he was a New Englander, but his antecedents were a bit vague. It was conceded that he had been born in Boston. Where he had been and what he had been between that event and his arrival in Carlshafen were not known. Sterns did not talk a great deal about himself, but he did intimate that he had traveled extensively, both in America and on the Continent, where he had come into contact with Prince Carl.

Papa Rosenthal glanced up at his visitor and nodded. "Howdy, Mark," he said. "Sit down; what's on your mind?"

Sterns sat down, folding his bony hands across his stomach.

"Rosenthal," he said in a high-pitched nasal voice, "I understand you've been offering your wagons to transport the colonists."

"Reckon that's correct," Papa agreed.

"Well," said Sterns, "you haven't any right to

do it. I'm handling that business, and I don't want you to horn in."

"The way you've been handling it, it's about time somebody horned in, as you put it," Rosenthal replied acidly.

Sterns' eyes narrowed a trifle. "I've got a contract to handle that business," he said. "Stick your nose in and you're liable to have a lawsuit on your hands."

"Sue and be damned to you!" growled Papa. "I'm thinking of human lives, not dollars and cents."

Sterns leaned forward and spoke softly. "It's just possible that something might happen to you if you don't lay off," he said.

Cameron decided he had heard enough. He stepped from the back room, his cold eyes fixed on Sterns' face. Sterns looked surprised and a little startled. Cameron regarded him a moment in silence, and when he spoke his voice was quiet but had a hard, metallic edge to it.

"Sterns, I heard what you said, and I'm here to call your hand. If you and Fitch and his bunch of murdering drygulchers are looking for trouble, you can find it till it runs out of your ears."

Sterns winced a little beneath the cowboy's

hard stare.

"Cameron, what you just said is unwarranted and distinctly slanderous," he replied.

"The truth is never unwarranted, and it's darned difficult to slander a skunk," Cameron answered. "Sterns, I've put my cards on the table, and you can look for me any time you want to, but lay off others. If you don't—well, heaven help you, Sterns, if I come to get you!"

Mark Sterns was no coward, but he shrank back in his chair before the cold fire in the speaker's eyes. He didn't know it, but he was looking at the face of one of the feuding Camerons of Calvert Valley who, outnumbered ten to one, had nevertheless fought the McPhersons to a bloody standstill.

"If you have anything more to say, say it quick," Cameron added. "If you haven't, get out!"

Sterns got out, hurriedly. At the door he turned his head to shoot a murderous glance at the cowboy; then he was gone. Cameron sat down and began rolling a cigarette.

"Well, you told him, boy," chuckled Papa Rosenthal, his eyes snapping.

"Yes, there was nothing else to do," Cameron

said. "If we'd given in and let him buffalo us, the advantage would all have been his. I expect we're likely to have a fight on our hands, but I've a notion we can give them as good as they send."

"Yes, we'll fight," Papa said.

Cameron nodded. He had no doubts about Papa Rosenthal. The mild little man in the chair had dared a stormy sea and the dangers and privations of a wild frontier land to seek and find the things that were more precious to his kind than life itself—freedom of thought, freedom of expression, freedom to worship according to the dictates of his own conscience, and the privilege of self-government. He would have scant patience with men who cared nothing for the things he revered. Sterns and Fitch would face a formidable opponent in the one-time *schlager* fighter.

Papa glanced out the window again. "Here comes Rivercomb," he announced. A moment later the lanky old ranch owner entered the office.

"Howdy, Papa," he said. "What you doing here, Rance? The south pasture is supposed to be combed today. Oh, I forgot; you quit a while back, didn't you? Hadn't noticed. Just as much work left undone as usual. Understand you're figuring to get married and settle down."

"Who the devil told you that?" Cameron demanded.

"Nobody. Just heard you rode off with a mighty purty gal in your arms, so what else is to be expected? Well, when Papa gets fed up with you, come on back to the spread. I'm feeling charitable, and the girl has to eat and have a roof over her head. Maybe in four or five years I can teach you how to be a range boss, but I ain't overly hopeful."

He sat down, stuffed a black old pipe with blacker tobacco, regarding Cameron the while with his snapping little black eyes. He got the pipe going to suit him and abruptly dropped his bantering tone.

"Understand you had a run-in or two with Fitch and his hellions," he said.

"I had a run-in with Fitch in the Best Chance, but I have no proof that Fitch had anything to do with the other things that happened," Cameron replied.

Rivercomb nodded his head. "He's a hard one to get proof against," he said, "but sooner or later he'll slip. I'm just waiting for that time, and I'm all set to pull on the rope. Hear he's been getting chummy with Mark Sterns. I met Sterns down the street. He was mumblin' and grumblin' to himself like he had the toothache. Passed by without even seeing me. Wonder what happened to him?"

Papa Rosenthal told him. Rivercomb didn't appear particularly surprised.

"Another slick-iron gent, or I miss my guess," he said. "Well, we've got plenty of ropes.

"But you want to look out for that pair," he added. "They're bad. Fitch will stop at nothing, and I wouldn't be surprised if Sterns is one of the same brand. Fact is, I consider him the more dangerous of the two; he's got more brains. Well, it sounds like it ought to be a nice row all around and I want to get in it, so I'm sending over three wagons with some of my old work dodgers to drive 'em, Papa. They're so old and spavined up they just hanker to get shot. Never mind gabbin' about it now; you ain't going to keep me out. Fact is, I'm liable to go along with Rance, if he's taking the ride up to New Braunfels. He has to have somebody along to do his thinking for him. He's likely as not to forget where he's headed and to take the fork to San Antonio."

He stood up, unfolding his lanky six-feet-two by degrees, waved away Papa's thanks and strode to the door.

"Going up to Rafferty's to get pizened," he said over his shoulder. "The stuff that hellion takes money for! Cactus spines and rattlesnake juice, but it packs a wallop."

"I feel better," said Papa, after the ranch owner had clumped out. "A mighty good man to have working with you, none better."

"And he's itching for a crack at Fitch," Rance added. "He's convinced Fitch has been wide-looping his cows and killed one of his night hawks. Anybody else would have been yelling for the Rangers, but not old Jim; he prefers to skin his own skunks."

Cameron spent most of the day helping Papa Rosenthal. Late in the evening he stopped at the Best Chance for a drink, something to eat and a few words with Rafferty. He was in an equable frame of mind, for it looked as if things would work out satisfactorily. He did not see Lije Fitch arrive at Carlshafen on a lathered horse, powdered with dust and in a hellish temper.

CHAPTER XII

Fitch skirted the main portion of the town to reach the house where Mark Sterns lived and had his office.

"Well, what else have you managed to bungle?" the agent greeted him acidly.

Fitch swore and glowered, but Sterns didn't appear impressed.

"Sit down and have a drink," he invited; "you look as if you need it."

Fitch gulped a glass of raw whiskey as if it were so much water and poured another.

"What's happened here since I left?" he growled.

"Plenty," Sterns replied. "Rosenthal is horning in and offering transportation to the Dutchies. He can't handle many, but enough to maybe make trouble. Cameron is working with him, and I've reason to believe Jim Rivercomb is too. Three of his wagons are in town with three of his salty old gunfighters driving them and a couple more along for good measure. If you hadn't bungled your chore, all this wouldn't have happened. Cameron would have been out of the picture."

Fitch appeared on the verge of an explosion, but instead he downed another drink, refilled his glass and grinned evilly.

"Speaking of Cameron, I've got some news for you," he said. "I got in touch with our fellow up at New Braunfels. He told me Cameron and Solms-Braunfels were getting along like two ticks on a sheep's back. They had quite a few talks, and then all of a sudden Cameron lit out for here. I'm just wondering if maybe Solms-Braunfels has been getting a notion or two about you and has sent Cameron here to do a little nosing around. If he finds out what became of most of the money Solms-Braunfels trusted you to handle, you may have some explaining to do."

It was Sterns' turn to flush and glower. "How was I to figure a war would start building up and scramble everything?" he demanded.

"You should have known it," Fitch countered. "I told you it would happen, sure as shooting, if annexation came. But no, you said the oilers wouldn't fight, that they had more sense than to commit suicide. Well, unless all signs fail they're going to fight, and mighty soon. So all the freighters you had arrangements with are going back on you, eh?"

"Yes, but if you hadn't slipped up on the chore I handed you it wouldn't matter. Not only did you let Cameron reach the prince, but you let fifty thousand dollars slip through your fingers."

"How did I know there was going to be a loco slip-up like that?" yelled Fitch. "I had everything planned perfect. It was that infernal Cameron who caught on, I'll bet money. If I'd known in time he was going along, I'd have told the boys to be more careful and maybe use some other method. It must have been Rosenthal's idea, him going along at the last minute. I tell you everything was planned perfect. The men would have been killed and the girl would have reported that Indians raided the wagon. How Cameron caught on is beyond me, but he did. Nolan, the only one of those no-goods who didn't get mowed down, said that when they headed for the wagon lead began flying from the brush in every direction. Sounded like a dozen men were shooting, only they knew there couldn't be more than three. They figured that after the boys who had the chore of grabbing off the stuff were cashed in, the hellions' guns would be empty. They made a try from the far side of the creek, and ran into a powder factory."

"And those stupid hellions I hired to do. for Cameron on his way back from New Braunfels! What do *they* do! They let Cameron lead 'em on and run smack into an ambush and get blown from under their hats. I came nigh to shooting one that escaped when the three of them came back and tried to bluster it out. The feather-brained dolts I have to work with! No wonder that blasted Cameron is still sashaying around. All he has to do is let the loco horned toads fall over their own feet and bust their own necks!"

"You didn't have much luck with him your-self when you tangled with him in Rafferty's," Stens remarked pointedly.

If Sterns had expected to get another explosion from Fitch he was disappointed. When Fitch replied his voice was quiet, his manner calculat-ing.

"You're right," he admitted. "He got the drop on me, all right. He handles that new-fangled gun of his mighty fast."

"Perhaps you should get one of that type," Sterns observed.

Fitch shook his head. "I don't like them," he replied. "I tried one out, but that turning cylinder makes me nervous. I couldn't hit the side of a house with the thing. My old single-barrel isn't so fast and has only one slug to throw out, but when I pull the trigger I don't miss. All I ask is a chance to pull trigger first. And I'll get it, don't worry about that."

He gulped his drink and tipped the bottle again.

"If you guzzled less of that stuff maybe you'd be better off," Sterns remarked. "Well, there's no sense in us yapping at each other. What's done is done, and quarreling over it won't help. And there's more money coming. I've got it on good authority that Baron Hans von Meusebach is on his way to replace Solms-Braunfels as commissioner-general for the Society, and he'll be plenty heeled."

"Maybe a raid on the infernal fort at New Braunfels would pay off," Fitch observed.

"Ought to be some good picking there."

"Not now; too well defended," Sterns replied. "But later it may be a notion. When Solms-Braunfels pulls out, most of the bunch there will pull out with him. And I think he'll pull out even before von Meusebach arrives here; they don't get along, and I think he doesn't want to meet him. Solms-Braunfels will leave the money behind. He wouldn't bother to take it along. It's small potatoes to him; he's one of the richest men in Germany. After he's gone, we'll see."

"I still can't understand how Cameron come to deal himself cards in the game," grumbled Fitch. "I know he planned to head west when he left here."

"Understand there's a woman mixed up in it," Sterns observed dryly.

Fitch nodded.

"Sterns," he asked softly, "just what spread did you once ride for?"

"That's my business," Sterns replied shortly.

"Uh-huh, reckon it is," Fitch conceded, "but I wouldn't be surprised if some sheriffs and maybe the Rangers would figure it's their business, too," he added with an evil grin.

Sterns glared at him and didn't answer.

"The question is," he said at length, "what are we going to do about Cameron? He's the real trouble-maker in this business."

Fitch tensed. An expression of vindictiveness set the hard lines in his face even harder.

"I'm figuring out something for him," he answered. "I got a score to even with that hombre, and I aim to even it. Let me handle him."

"Okay, but be careful," Sterns warned. "He's a cold proposition, and he's got brains. Make one slip with him and you're a goner. I've a notion he's got a score to settle with you, too, and don't forget about Jim Rivercomb while you're at it. Rivercomb never forgets and never forgives. I know he hasn't got anything on you, but let him make up his own mind for sure about certain things and that'll be enough for him; he'll act. We've got a couple of hard men arrayed against us, Fitch, with Rosenthal to help them think things out."

"I've gone up against hard men before now," growled Fitch. Sterns nodded and did not comment.

"Well, I'm going to get something to eat," Fitch said, standing up and wiping his lips.

"Better stay away from Rafferty's place,"

Sterns cautioned. "Cameron and maybe River-comb are likely to be there, and you're quick at getting your bristles up. Nothing to be gained by looking for trouble right now. If you go off half-cocked you'll spoil everything."

"Okay," Fitch conceded grudgingly, "I'll keep away from the Best Chance. The very sight of that hellion makes me see red."

After Fitch had taken his departure, Sterns locked the door and made sure the shutters were closed. He crossed to a big iron safe standing in a corner of the room and opened it. He took out packets of bank notes and riffled them with his fingers. In his eyes was the hot glow of uncontrolled avarice.

Putting the money back, he took something from a shelf. It was a Colt revolver of the latest pattern, similar to the one Rance Cameron carried. He examined it a moment, replaced it and shut the safe door. He filled a glass with whiskey and held it to the light.

"Here's to them killing one another, after a while," he said aloud, and tossed off the drink.

CHAPTER XIII

Cameron ate dinner in the Best Chance at a table near a window through which the night air blew pleasantly. Rafferty, who seemed to know about everything that went on, came over to the table.

"Lije Fitch is in town," he said. "He's down at the Lavaca having something to eat and considerable more to drink. 'Pears he's in a bad temper over something."

"Did you get a look at him?"

"No, I wasn't down there. Tom Doran saw him and told me. Said he thought I'd like to know."

Cameron nodded, not particularly interested. It was logical that Fitch would return to Carlshafen as soon as his business in San Antonio was completed. It was equally logical that he would proceed to get drunk. He wondered idly if Fitch had seen the three bodies in the trail and what he thought about it. He had very likely been told they were there by the drygulchers who had escaped. Fitch's remarks must have been worth listening to.

After he finished eating, Cameron sat toying with a cigarette and studying his surroundings. The scene was familiar enough—he had viewed it a hundred times—but tonight it had a vague unreality. He puzzled over the phenomenon until the explanation dawned: he was a stranger here. He had been gone only a few days, not months or years, but he had returned a stranger. He was no longer an integral part of his surroundings.

The answer? It was not slow in coming: a woman. She had wrought the change in him, had opened up new vistas.

He was recalled to prosaic reality by a hand on his shoulder. Rafferty was beside him.

"Come over to the end of the bar, away from that window," the saloonkeeper urged.

"Why?" Cameron asked.

"Come over to the end of the bar," Rafferty

repeated. "I'll explain then."

Cameron shrugged and followed him to the far end of the bar, next to the stockroom, where nobody was standing.

"Now what's up?" he asked.

"One of Fitch's men came in a little while ago," Rafferty replied in a low voice.

"Well?"

"He came in, had a drink and looked all around careful like he was hunting for somebody. Then he slid out."

"Nothing unusual about that."

"Maybe not," Rafferty conceded, "but the way things have been going of late, it made me sort of curious. I told Tom Doran, who was having a drink with me, to amble along after him and see where he went and what he did. He went right to the Lavaca and sat down with Fitch. Doran couldn't hear what was said, but he saw Fitch take out his pistol, look it over and put a fresh cap on the nipple. He hustled back here and told me."

"And—" Cameron prompted.

"And I figured right in front of a window opening onto a dark alley was no place for you to be settin'," Rafferty replied. "I wouldn't put anything past that snake-blooded buzzard."

Cameron nodded. "You' might be right." He was silent for a moment; then he said:

"I'm going to take a little walk; be seeing you."

"Rance," the saloonkeeper cautioned anxiously, "don't go looking for trouble."

"I'm not," Cameron answered; "neither am I sidestepping any that comes my way."

Outside the door, he glanced up and down the street; there was nobody in sight. He slipped into the alley, skirted the bar of light streaming through the window, stepped into a dark opening between two buildings and waited.

He didn't have long to wait. A few minutes later the form of a man materialized in the alley mouth, slunk along furtively, hugging the saloon wall, and crouched beneath the window. Cameron slipped from the opening and glided forward on noiseless feet.

Lije Fitch slowly straightened until he could peer across the window sill, which was just below the level of a tall man's eyes; the cocked pistol swung loosely in his right hand. He stiffened with a grunt as a voice spoke behind him.

"Looking for somebody, Lije?"

Fitch gurgled in his throat. He did not move, for he knew perfectly well that the thing pressing against his backbone was the cold, steely muzzle of a gun. "I—I wasn't looking for you," he stuttered. "I was just looking for one of my boys."

"A likely story," Cameron retorted. "Okay, I guess we'll have it out sooner or later, anyhow, so—" He stepped back a pace.

Fitch whirled, writhing sideways like a snake.

Cameron struck upward with his Colt, hard. The barrel clanged on metal. The pistol boomed and the bullet whizzed over his shoulder. With a yell of terror, Fitch wheeled and ran wildly down the alley. Cameron watched him go.

Inside the saloon was a sudden hush, then a babble of talk. Cameron walked quickly to the alley mouth and the street before anybody came out. When he reached the door, men were peering out cautiously.

"Where was the shootin'?" somebody asked.

"Down the alley, I'd say," Cameron replied, and entered the saloon.

Rafferty greeted him with an anxious face. "Was it Fitch?" he asked in barely audible tones.

"That's right," Cameron replied.

"Did he take a shot at you?"

"He missed."

"And you let him go?" Cameron nodded.

"You should have killed the son," Rafferty declared wrathfully. "You'll have to anyway, before things are finished, if he don't kill you."

"Guess you've got the right of it, John," Cameron agreed soberly. "Let's have a drink."

Shortly afterward, Cameron headed for bed. His introspective mood had evaporated and his mind was dealing only with cold facts. Quite likely Rafferty was right; he should have killed Fitch. But he still shrank from killing unless he was absolutely forced to. He had no desire for a return of the blood fever that had gripped him in Calvert Valley. He had traveled a thousand miles to get away from that and its consequences. Never again did he wish to take part in scenes such as he had witnessed—with bereaved women, fatherless children, destroyed homesteads. He wanted to live at peace with his fellow men, but it appeared he wasn't going to be allowed to.

There was a chance, he reflected, not very hopefully, that the scare Fitch had gotten might cause him to lay off. Rather unlikely, though;

he'd be more liable to look upon the mischance as just another count against him, Cameron, that was to be evened up when the opportunity afforded. Well, that could wait, and anyhow, there wasn't anything much he could do about it except try to stay alive.

Mark Sterns was aroused by a pounding on his front door. He got out of bed, put on a dressing gown and opened the door to admit Lije Fitch. One look at Fitch's contorted face was enough to inform him what had happened.

"So, you bungled again, I see," he remarked, closing and locking the door.

Fitch lurched to the table, grabbed the bottle resting on it and poured a brimming glass. He downed the whiskey at a gulp, and wiped his lips with the back of his hand.

"No, I didn't bungle," he said in a strained voice. "I was just outsmarted, that's all. Give the devil his due. That hellion has got plenty of wrinkles on his horns; he's as full of savvy as a tree's full of owls."

"All right, out with it," said Sterns. "Just what happened?"

Fitch told him, embellishing the story with

sulphurous profanity. "I don't know how he caught on, but he did," he concluded.

"If you hadn't been drunk you might have stopped to realize that he would be keeping tab on your movements," Sterns said. "He's got friends in this town, and they spotted you and kept him informed. It's a wonder he didn't shoot you instead of letting you go. Well, anyhow, I'm glad you didn't kill him."

"What!" Fitch stared at him, his eyes blinking.

"That's just what I said," Sterns repeated. "I'm glad you didn't kill him. I don't want him killed just yet; not the way you planned to do it. That's why I told you to stay away from the Best Chance, but as usual you didn't listen. Why didn't I want him killed? I'll tell you." He paused to help himself to a drink and continued.

"I didn't want Cameron killed just yet because I'm of the opinion that he possesses valuable information. Solms-Braunfels very likely discussed his plans with him, what he intends to do and how, and when. I want to know those plans. There's fifty thousand dollars—a lot more for that matter—at stake. I want a chance to make Cameron talk before he's killed."

"You think you can scare Cameron into talking?" Fitch sneered.

"No, I don't think I could scare him," Sterns admitted. "But there are ways to make a man talk. I am familiar with several. For instance, one I learned from the Chinese."

Fitch moved uncomfortably in his chair. He didn't seem able to meet Stern's glittering eyes; his own shifted nervously about the room.

"It's an interesting method," Sterns said. "The gentleman is tied hand and foot, so that he cannot move, not even his head. Over him a flask of water is suspended. There is a tiny hole in the bottom of the flask, through which a drop of water falls on his forehead every few seconds. After an hour of that, he'll tell you anything he knows."

Fitch's jaw sagged a little and he wet his lips with the tip of a nervous tongue.

"Then there's the death-of-ten-thousand-cuts," Sterns resumed. "A small hatchet is the instrument used. You start with the fingers and toes and continue chopping till the subject is ready to talk."

Sterns looked reflective, shook his head gently as if in mild wonder.

"Strange how tenacious life is," he observed. "I've seen a Chinese shaped like an egg, and his eyes still bright."

Lije Fitch was a hard man, but he shivered. "Listen," he growled, "if you've got something like that in mind, count me out. I'd like to kill that son and I'm going to if I get a chance, but I ain't torturing no man to death. You handle it."

Sterns shot him a contemptuous glance. "I'll handle it," he replied, "and I won't bungle the chore. And now I'm going to give you a bit of advice, and this time you'd better listen. Get out of town and stay out for a while. If the story of what happened tonight gets around you may find yourself in rather hot water. Killing a man in a fair fight is one thing; shooting him in the back in the dark is something else. People don't like that, not even in a tough town like this one. You just might find yourself the principal attraction at a necktie party. But public indignation doesn't continue to boil for long, and after a bit things will cool down and people will forget about it. Just keep out of sight for a while till they do cool down."

Fitch grumbled and swore but conceded that

Sterns might have the right of it.

"I'll stay out for a while," he promised.

"Okay, I'll keep in touch with you," Sterns said, "and I'll handle that little matter we were discussing in my own way."

Fitch shivered again, and departed rather hurriedly.

CHAPTER XIV

Cameron rose early, for he had decided to accompany the wagon train to New Braunfels. He felt he should lay what he had learned before the prince. Perhaps Solms-Braunfels could accomplish or suggest something to remedy the deplorable conditions in Carlshafen which Cameron knew would steadily and quickly worsen.

Ten wagons made up the train, a pitiful modicum of what was needed. They were loaded to capacity with men and women selected by Papa Rosenthal. He felt it best that no children should make the initial trip.

Driving the three vehicles donated by Jim Rivercomb were grizzled old waddies who could be relied on in any emergency. Three of the same brand lounged carelessly in their saddles, pacing the train and alert for anything that looked off-color.

Not that Cameron anticipated any serious difficulty on the way. The train was just a bit too well manned.

"What we want to do," Cameron told the men, "is make the best speed possible and hustle back for more loads. Those folks must be gotten out of Carlshafen as quickly as possible."

"The way they're living, they'll be lucky if cholera or yellow jack don't take a swipe at them," repeated Cliff Hardy, who had charge of the Walking R teamsters and riders. "Let's go; you work dodgers, try and keep awake from here to Victoria at least. I don't want anybody falling off his horse this trip."

The Walking R hands grinned, fully appreciating the joke. "Ain't it nice to think he'll be gone in another month or two?" observed one. "Then maybe we'll get somebody in his place that ain't all spavined up and terrapin-brained and knows his elbow from a hole in the ground." He winked at Rance as he spoke.

"You won't need to have any trouble with them, Rance," Hardy observed. "Just get yourself a good sheep dog to round 'em up and head 'em in the right direction. Anyhow, they'll always show up at the feed trough."

As Cameron expected, the trip to New Braunfels was without incident. The arrival of the train was unexpected, but the word spread quickly. Prince Carl and his aides hurried down from the fort to greet the colonists.

Cameron found Mary's greeting all that was to be desired. He was with her in the big hall when he received a summons from the prince.

He found Solms-Braunfels seated at his desk, fingering a sheet of paper upon which something was written. The prince waved him to a chair and looked expectant.

"Did you learn anything?" he asked, "and how is it that the people arrived in wagons owned by *Herr* Rosenthal and his friend the *Herr* Rivercomb, I believe it is?"

Cameron answered the first question first, incorporating his answer to the second.

"I learned this much, sir," he said. "I learned that your man Sterns is tied up with a murderous killer who is also suspected of smuggling and cattle stealing and who, I'm pretty sure, was implicated in the attempt on the wagon that transported the gold here. I also learned that Sterns has done absolutely nothing to arrange for transporting the people from Carlshafen and apparently has no intention of doing so."

Solms-Braunfels drummed on the desk top with his fingers. "Those are serious charges, *Herr* Cameron," he said.

Cameron's eyes flashed a little. "And they can be proven," he answered.

The prince nodded. He rose to his feet and began nervously pacing the room, his brow clouded, his lips moving as if in soundless speech. Cameron rolled a cigarette and watched him.

The prince ceased his pacing and turned to face Cameron.

"*Herr* Cameron," he said abruptly, "I am leaving New Braunfels."

"Yes?" Cameron was not particularly surprised.

"Yes," the prince repeated. "Annexation is now a fact. I cannot hope to deal with Washington as I have with the government of Texas. I am returning to Germany, where I will prepare to launch another project in another land. I have received word that my successor as commissioner-general for the Society is even now on his way here."

"And what about Sterns?" Cameron asked.

The prince shrugged. "Let von Meusebach deal with him as he sees fit. He is a man of short speech and, like yourself, he does not trust *Herr* Sterns. The problem is his, along with many others; let him cope with it."

He crossed to the desk and sat down, and his smile was almost whimsical.

"I have done what I could, to the best of my ability," he said. "I feel that I have done well. This community may suffer privation, may encounter great difficulties, but will, I firmly believe, survive and prosper. And I feel, *Herr* Cameron," the smile broadened, "that you will play an important part in its development—you and the lady who is to be your wife. It has been good to know you. I leave you with a heightened respect for America and all things American."

"You leave at once, sir?" Cameron asked as he rose to go.

"On the morrow I ride, with those who cling to me," Solms-Braunfels answered.

"To Carlshafen?"

"No, to Corpus Cristi, where I have arranged for a ship to put in," the prince replied. A touch of bitterness crept into his voice. "My successor may arrive at Carlshafen at any time now, and I prefer not to meet him."

He stood up, held out his hand. "I repeat, my son, it has been good to know you," he said. "May you live long and prosper."

Once again Cameron experienced a touch of sadness as he left Prince Carl's presence. He felt that he had looked upon the fragments of a shattered dream.

Mary was waiting for him in the hall. She evinced no surprise at what he had to tell her.

"Preparations for departure have been made for several days," she said. "It is an open secret that my uncle believed that annexation would not tend to further his plans. And to tell the truth, he is tired of New Braunfels. It is his nature. The excitement of launching a project is one thing, the prosaic business of developing it another. He yearns for fresh fields, new beginnings. He'll always be like that, but I really believe he does good."

"He does," Cameron replied. "Are all the others going with him?"

"Not all," she answered. "Johan remains. The prince has turned over to him the administration of affairs here until Baron von Meusebach arrives. And Henry also remains, and a few others who were mixed up in political intrigue and feel that it would not be wise for them to return to Germany at the present."

"And Count Otto?" he asked teasingly.

"Oh, Otto is overjoyed. He longs for the flesh pots of civilization. He'll run his road to whatever end is appointed for his sort, and always joyously. Good luck to him!"

Cameron also wished the happy-go-lucky young nobleman good luck when the time came to say goodbye.

"It I shall need," Count Otto said cheerfully. "It I always need, and I trust it will not me fail. *Herr Teufel* looks after his own, *ja?*"

Cameron chuckled and felt that the Devil would look after Count Otto. Doubtless even Satan himself wouldn't be able to keep from liking the sunny-natured young rapscallion.

Cameron did not speak with Prince Carl again. The following morning he watched him ride away, sitting his horse as a cavalryman should, his plumed soldiers following, backs ramrod-stiff, eyes to the front. Light wagons bore the ladies of his comic opera court. Cameron watched them till they vanished into the mists of the distance like brightly colored leaves on the wings of an autumn wind. Yes, the gay-hued leaves were gone, but the tree, thrusting its roots deeper and deeper in the willing soil, remained.

Mary handed him an unsealed envelope. "His parting gift to you," she said. "He feared your American pride would not allow you to accept it if he proffered it himself."

Cameron examined the envelope's contents and whistled—a thousand dollars in bills of large denominations! He replaced the money, grinned and handed it back to Mary. "Keep it," he said.

"But why?" she demurred. "It's yours."

"I was taught that a family gets along better if the wife handles the money," he replied. "Tuck it away till you need some to buy a cradle with. What's the matter? Your face is the color of a sunset."

Hand in hand they walked slowly up the hill to the fort. The great hall was silent and empty. Sunlight streaming through the windows dappled the floor with gold, but in the corners shadows clustered.

Mary shivered. "It's full of ghosts!" she declared. "Let's find Johan and Henry."

They found them in the little room off the kitchen, with filled mugs at their elbows and a steaming joint on the table between them.

Cameron chuckled at the change in their appearance. Gone were the ornate uniforms and the gold braid. Both wore overalls and blue cotton shirts, glaringly new. They rose to their feet as Mary entered, but she waved them back to their chairs.

"We'll join you, if we may," she said.

"We're well on the way to becoming Texans," Henry chuckled as he wielded a knife on the joint. "Johan is already talking dams and irrigation and cattle. Bet they elect him mayor when things really get going."

Later the others of the prince's following who had remained behind joined them. They appeared rather sad and depressed at first, but perked up considerably under the influence of a few mugs and Henry's cheerful chatter. One of the women was the young Baroness Frieda Houthem, who was a widow. Cameron decided that Henry wouldn't have much difficulty making her forget Count Otto.

The wagons stayed over another day to allow the horses to rest and then headed back to the coast.

"I'll be seeing you soon," Cameron told Mary. "Johan and Henry will look after you. Maybe we'll bring the baron with us when we come back. The prince spoke as if he would arrive in Carlshafen any day. Do you know him?"

"Yes," she replied. "He's stern and soldierly, but a good man. He will do what he can. Be careful and take care of yourself, my darling. I'll be waiting."

Cameron rode back to Carlshafen in a cheerful mood. Doubtless Baron von Meusebach would arrive shortly and take charge of the situation. Mark Sterns, he believed, was in for a very unpleasant interview with the German nobleman. With everything under control, he would be free to return to the Walking R. He knew Cliff Hardy was anxious to relinquish the responsibilities of range boss and attend to the details of taking over his property. Yes, it looked as if things were going to work out.

They didn't. When he arrived at Carlshafen he learned from Papa Rosenthal that so far there was no word from the baron. It was evident that he had taken ship, but the stormy Atlantic was no respecter of persons and carried on as it pleased no matter who was endeavoring to plow through its turbulent waters.

However, it had not stopped or delayed the immigrant ships. Three more had arrived during Cameron's absence. Papa Rosenthal was toiling night and day to provide food and shelter for the newcomers. He had managed by some miracle to get hold of four more wagons.

"But they're coming faster than we can move them," he told Cameron. "Sterns? He has done nothing and evidently doesn't intend to do anything. He refuses to see me and sent word that his plans are none of my business. A delegation from the settlement went to see him and could learn nothing definite. He told them he was endeavoring to arrange transportation, complained at great length about the difficulties the war preparations placed in his way and assured them he was doing all he could. He is doing nothing."

Cameron nodded. He rather expected to hear any day that Sterns had pulled out. He doubted if he had any desire to come to grips with von

Meusebach. Well, there was nothing to be done about it.

"Fitch hasn't been seen in town since you left," Rosenthal added. "His wagons are freighting army supplies. I don't think we have anything more to worry about where he's concerned. You evidently scared him good. Yes, I heard about it; Rafferty told me. He's still fuming because you didn't shoot Fitch when you had the chance. I am a man of peace, but maybe Rafferty has the right notion."

Cameron chuckled, but he did not agree with Papa that they had nothing more to fear from Fitch. He was confident that Fitch had something in mind and that it would turn out to be something unpleasant. Well, whatever it was, it would be taken care of when it happened, one way or another. He dismissed Fitch and busied himself helping Rosenthal get another train for New Braunfels under way.

But Papa decided that before dispatching another convoy, he would use the wagons to freight in lumber and provisions, there being a woeful lack of both.

The colonists did their own building, many of the men being experienced and thoroughly com-

petent in such matters. They quickly threw together the rough shacks to provide temporary
housing. There was no attempt at permanency,
for all expected to move on to New Braunfels
in a very short time.

They were a sturdy, cheerful and industrious
lot. Texas was lucky to get them, Cameron
thought.

But as he rode across the hot, damp lowlands,
with the fierce sun glaring overhead, he experienced an uneasy foreboding that refused to be
downed. This was not a good place for people
from a cooler clime to live, especially under such
deplorable sanitary conditions. Well, perhaps
they would soon all be in New Braunfels where
the climate was more salubrious. Or so he hoped.

The blazing July days brought torrential rains
but no lessening of the torrid heat. When the
sky was clear, one roasted; when it rained, one
steamed.

"I reckon next we'll get a hurricane," John
Rafferty predicted disgustedly. "I never saw
such an infernal summer."

With lumber and provisions for their imme-
diate needs provided, the wagons rolled again,
every available inch of space utilized. And still

von Meusebach had not put in an appearance.

Cameron found Johan and Henry working like beavers to make preparations for the new arrivals and the many more to come. Johan was worried over the non-arrival of the baron.

"I like not the responsibility," he confided to Cameron. "Prince Carl left the gold in my care, and it is a great sum. It is to meet the final payment on the land and many other things."

"Guess it's safe enough here," Cameron comforted him.

"Perhaps," Johan conceded doubtfully, "but I keep a close watch on it. I wish the baron would come."

Mary wanted to accompany him when they prepared to return to Carlshafen, but Cameron said no.

"You're better off here," he told her. "It's a lot cooler and not so humid. Besides," he added, "Johan and Henry need somebody to cheer them up."

"Henry doesn't need any cheering up," Mary sniffed. "Frieda Houthem is seeing to that. Watching them together makes me darn lonesome."

Shortly after leaving New Braunfels, Cameron rode on alone. He was anxious to get back to Carlshafen, and he could make the trip in less than a third of the time required by the lumbering vehicles.

Swiftly, tirelessly the great blue horse forged ahead, his steady gait eating up the miles. The sun crossed the zenith and drifted down the long slant of the western sky.

Cameron made a fireless camp, eating sparingly of some cold food he carried along with the staple provisions in his saddle pouches, washing it down with water from a little stream. A vast depression had settled upon him, and he did not feel like making an effort to cook something more substantial. For a while he lay gazing up at the hot stars and finally fell into a troubled sleep.

Dawn found him on the move, his eyes fixed on the ever retreating skyline that would not come to rest until he saw the blue waters of the bay. He paused briefly at Victoria and headed into the wild country to the south. The sense of foreboding had strengthened, and he was obsessed by an uncontrollable urge to bring the journey to a quick conclusion. His habitual caution was dulled, and he rode careless of his surroundings.

Otherwise he might have correctly interpreted the faint rustling in the growth that flanked the trail, and in time. As it was, the tight loop that snaked from the brush fell over his head, settled around his shoulders and was instantly jerked tight, hurling him to the ground with stunning force. Before he could make a move, three men swarmed out of the chaparral and whipped the rope around and around his body, securing it with a double hitch and rendering him utterly helpless.

"Catch that horse, Jenks," ordered a bearded individual who appeared to be the leader of the trio.

The man called Jenks approached Smoke, who had continued a few paces before halting to gaze back, snorting inquiringly. Smoke stood perfectly still till Jenks reached for his bridle; then the gleaming teeth struck home, and Jenks leaped back with a howl of pain, gripping his blood-streaming arm. Smoke launched a vicious kick that missed, snorted and dashed into the brush, his hoofbeats swiftly fading away.

"Let the blue devil go," called the bearded man. "Oh, shut up; you ain't killed. You're lucky those irons didn't connect with you, or you'd be in Boot Hill right now and with something really to yelp about. Shut up and come on; we've got to get out of here."

Cameron was jerked to his feet. Still partially dazed by the force of his fall, he stumbled after the bearded man who held the end of the rope. The cursing Jenks and a bulky individual the bearded man addressed as Porter followed, shoving Cameron along roughly when he lagged.

The bearded man led him to where three horses were tethered. He swung into the saddle of one.

"All right," he told the captive, "walk or be drug, it's all one to me. Come along, you fellers; we're wasting time."

Cameron walked; there was nothing else to do. To offer resistance would be futile, even to ask questions a waste of time. He could only follow where his captors led. His mind was clearing, and he began taking stock of the situation. His conclusions were far from satisfactory; it was not difficult to perceive the hand of Lije Fitch or Mark Sterns in the affair. What puz-

zled him most was why he hadn't immediately
received a slug through the head. Well, he supposed he should be thankful that he had not. Or
should he? He experienced a very uncomfortable
premonition that what was in store for him
would be even more unpleasant. He would not
be left alive, but it was quite likely that before
his captors got through with him, he would welcome a chance to die. Just why had they kept
him alive so far? He hadn't the slightest notion,
unless it was from a sadistic desire to watch him
die in as horrible a fashion as they could con-
trive.

For nearly a mile Cameron trudged along
painfully behind the horses; the afternoon was
well advanced and the shadows were lengthen-
ing when he sighted a small, weather-beaten
cabin·in a clearing surrounded by chaparral.
Very likely the abandoned home of some pros-
pector or trapper; there were more than a few
such in the section, most of them very old and
long unoccupied.

The shack, however, showed signs of recent
tenancy; the door was closed, but a wisp of smoke
rose from the stick-and-mud chimney. There was
a lean-to over to one side, with bundles of forage

stacked under it and mangers for horses.

His captors rode straight for the door of the cabin and dismounted. Two of the horses were led to the lean-to, the third left standing in front of the cabin. Then one of the men opened the door and Cameron was shoved into the single room.

From the inside the place showed signs of occupancy. There were bunks built against the walls, on which were tumbled blankets. A table solidly constructed of thick planks stood in the center of the room, and several rough but sturdy chairs. A fire smoldered in a rusty stove on which rested several pots and a large coffee boiler. Shelves were stacked with staple provisions and bottles. To all appearances the cabin was an outlaw hideaway.

The bearded man gestured to a chair beside the table.

"Set down there," he ordered. Cameron obeyed.

"Porter, you set on the other side and keep your pistol handy," the bearded man continued. "Keep a sharp eye on this hellion; he's tricky."

"Going to untie him?" grunted Porter as he sat down and drew his weapon.

"Might as well," the other replied, adding with an evil laugh, "Want him to be in good shape when the Boss gets here. A strong and healthy feller lasts longer, you know, and is a heap more entertaining." He laughed again, and Cameron felt cold along his backbone.

"Reckon you got the notion, all right, Barney," Porter said, leering across the table at the prisoner. "Get the rope off him."

"You got his gun, but I'll make sure he ain't got another one cached somewhere," Barney said. He went over Cameron with expert hands but discovered no further arm. Cameron's second Colt was in his saddle pouch, and it might as well have been out in the Gulf for all the good it would do him, he reflected ruefully. He knew Smoke would follow to the clearing and remain nosing about in the brush, but that was small comfort under the circumstances.

Barney proceeded to unhitch the rope and flip it away, freeing Cameron's arms from its numbing constrictions.

"Put your hands on the table and keep 'em there," Barney commanded.

Cameron did so. Porter drew his pistol and held it with the barrel resting against the edge of the table.

"That's right," said Barney. "Now I'm going to fetch the Boss; should be back in a couple of hours or so. Keep an eye on that jigger; I tell you he's tricky."

"I'll take care of him, don't you worry," Porter growled.

"If anything goes wrong, *you'll* be the one to worry," Barney told him significantly. "So long."

The door closed behind him. A moment later Cameron heard the beat of hoofs drawing away from the cabin. He spoke for the first time.

"Well, what's the idea of all this?" he asked Porter.

"You'll find out," Porter replied. "The Boss will want to ask you a few questions while you're still able to answer them."

"And if I refuse to answer?"

"Oh, you'll answer all right," Porter said. "The Boss has ways of making fellers talk. I've watched him work over a few, and they talked; glad of the chance to."

Cameron digested Porter's remarks in silence. He wondered what information Fitch, or whoever the Boss was, wanted. However, he didn't wonder as to what fate was in store for him. That was painfully obvious. Death for sure, and very likely a lot of unpleasantness preceding it. He knew perfectly well he'd never be allowed to leave the cabin alive, and he was familiar enough with the cruelties sometimes practiced in the border country to make the prospect one of terror.

To one thing he firmly made up his mind: he was not going to allow himself to be tortured. But he hoped he might escape the ordeal without committing "suicide." The question was, how? On the face of things, escape appeared impossible. He had already catalogued Porter and Jenks as being rather stupid, slow-thinking individuals. Jenks was probably the more alert of the two, but there was no lack of vigilance on the part of the bulky man seated on the other side of the table with his pistol ready for instant action. His own Colt, he noticed, was thrust under Porter's belt, on the left side. Jenks wore two horse pistols.

The only thing he could do was watch for the slightest relaxation of the pair's watchfulness and take advantage of it. If he could manage to get hold of one of the guns he might have a fighting chance, but how to get hold of one was a problem. As the minutes slipped past with disturbing swiftness, the solution of the problem appeared more and more hopeless.

"Heat up that coffee, Jenks," Porter said at length. "I could stand a cup about now."

Still muttering over his lacerated arm, around which he had bound a handkerchief, Jenks moved to the stove and began building up the fire. He moved the coffee pot to a more favorable position and took down a couple of tin cups from a shelf. Cameron, sitting with his hands on the table, watched idly. Porter lounged comfortably in his chair, his slitted eyes fixed on the prisoner. Cameron pondered a method to cause his captors to relax their guard somewhat. He began to feign nervousness, blinking his eyes, twitching his lips, raking the table top with jerky nails. Porter watched him with malicious satisfaction. Cameron continued to pretend. Not that it was all pretense. His nerves were really strained to the breaking point, which under the circumstances was not unnatural.

"What do you suppose the Boss intends to do with me?" he asked, causing his voice to tremble a little.

Porter uttered an evil chuckle. "You'll find out," he replied. "Didn't I tell you the Boss is tops at making fellers talk? I've known one to talk so you could hear him a mile, when he was working him over."

Cameron wet his lips with his tongue and continued to simulate growing nervousness and apprehension, from which his captors evidently derived great pleasure. Porter chuckled again and relaxed in his chair, allowing his gun barrel to sway sideways a trifle. Jenks, still puttering about the stove, grinned over his shoulder at Cameron. He turned to a shelf and took down a bottle and held it to the light.

"What do you say to a little snort?" he suggested, shaking the bottle invitingly.

Porter looked a bit doubtful. "Okay," he said at length, "Only we got to take it easy. You know the Boss will raise ned if he catches us drinking when there's work to do."

"We'll go easy," Jenks said, picking up the two tin cups and placing them on the table at Porter's elbow.

"How about letting me have one?" Cameron asked thickly.

Jenks cast an inquiring glance at Porter as he

tipped the bottle over one of the cups.

"Oh, let him have one," said Porter. "Reckon he sort of needs it.' Jenks nodded and fetched another cup which he proceeded to fill. Porter picked it up with his free hand.

"You keep your hands right where they are," he cautioned Cameron. "And don't try to slosh it in my eyes," he added with a flash of shrewdness. "One funny move and I'll let you have it. Keep your hands right where they are."

Cameron had his hands where he wanted them, flat on the table top, his thumbs hooked under the edge of the thick plank. Porter raised the cup.

"I'll hold it to your mouth and let you drink," he said. "Easy, now."

He leaned forward, the table edge pressing against his short ribs. Jenks turned to replace the bottle on the shelf, pausing at the stove an instant.

With every ounce of his strength, Cameron shoved the table with an upward, wrenching twist. Porter's breath exhaled in a mighty whoosh as the table edge jammed hard against his middle. Over he went, chair and all, with a prodigious crash, the upended table half on top of him. Cameron shot out of his chair in a streaking dive and caught Porter as he came off the floor, gasping curses. Porter's pistol exploded so close that the flame seared Cameron's cheek and he felt the wind of the passing bullet. His arm clamped around Porter's neck and under his chin, whirled the bulky body around toward Jenks who, trying to replace the bottle on the shelf and draw his pistol at the same time, fumbled a fatal second. He got the pistol out and fired blindly as Cameron swung Porter around.

Porter screamed as the heavy slug tore through his body and smashed Cameron a terrific blow in the ribs. Cameron gasped, tottered, but whipped the Colt from under Porter's belt and fired at Jenks again and again. Jenks' second pistol exploded, but the bullet went wild. He stumbled forward with a choking cough and pitched onto his face. Porter's sagging body slipped from Cameron's grasp and thudded to the floor, where he lay breathing in choking gulps.

Cameron staggered against the wall and hung there for a moment. It felt as if his whole side had been torn out, but his exploring fingers found only a slight furrow in the flesh over his ribs; the slug had merely grazed them, but with enough force very nearly to knock him out. He clutched at the wall with his free hand, his cocked gun ready for action, and held on till his strength returned.

Jenks was dead. Porter was dying, his life draining out through his shattered lungs. Even as Cameron staggered to him, he gave a gurgling groan and lay still. Cameron holstered his gun, righted the overturned table and leaned on it for support.

The coffee boiled over with a hiss. Cameron straightened up from the table, stumbled to the stove and moved the pot off the glowing lid. With a trembling hand he poured a tin cup full and drank it as fast as the heat would allow. He refilled the cup, took that one a bit slower and felt somewhat better.

Cameron had but a vague notion as to how long Barney had been gone from the cabin. It seemed only a short while, but he could be mistaken. Also, Barney and his companion, or companions, might return sooner than anticipated. He wasn't feeling anything like his normal self and decided he'd do well to get out of there in a hurry. With a last glance at the outlaws, he left the cabin, closing the door behind him. Yes, he'd better be moving without delay. He was in no shape for a desperate encounter with two and possibly more men. Things had worked out a lot better than he had hoped for. No sense in playing his luck too strong.

The twilight was deepening and the shadows were already curdled thick under the trees. He glanced around, whistled a loud, clear note. A moment later there was a crashing in the brush and Smoke appeared, snorting inquiringly, and trotted to him. Cameron stroked his glossy neck and rubbed his velvety muzzle. Smoke nibbled his fingers and blew softly through his nose.

"Good boy!" Cameron said. "I knew you'd be hanging around waiting for me. Looked for a while like you'd have a heck of a long wait. Let's get out of here before something else cuts loose."

He mounted the moros and gave him his head, knowing that he would find the way to the trail.

Smoke diagonaled through the growth, picking his way carefully in the deepening darkness, and it was some time before he reached the trail.

Cameron rode warily, every sense on the alert. But either it had taken Barney longer than he had expected to locate the mysterious Boss or the pair had traveled to the cabin by a different route. Cameron met nobody on the trail and arrived at Carlshafen a couple of hours before dawn. Completely exhausted, he provided for all of Smoke's needs, tumbled into bed and was almost instantly asleep.

He awoke stiff and sore, his bruised ribs still painful, but otherwise none the worse for wear. He repaired to the restaurant for something to eat and then gave considerable thought to the happenings of the day before, finally deciding there was nothing much to be done about the incident. He couldn't very well confront Fitch and Sterns and accuse them of being responsible. Cameron was convinced that one or the other was. Very likely both had had a hand in the business. But just the same he had not an iota of proof to back up an accusation. He'd just have to let the matter pass, and be more careful in the future, having learned to respect the devilish ingenuity and utter ruthlessness of his enemies.

Cameron found Papa Rosenthal badly worried. "I fear what may happen to people accustomed to living under sanitary conditions, many of whom were gently reared and have never known hardship," he said. "Sterns refuses to do anything to better conditions, which are steadily worsening. Feeling against him is running high, but he doesn't seem to mind, contending that he can do nothing at the present because of the difficulties presented by the war preparations and his inability to hold the teamsters to their contracts."

"Might help some to hang him," Cameron growled.

"There are others who hold similar views," Rosenthal conceded.

In the days that followed, Cameron kept a close watch for the bearded man called Barney, but saw neither hide nor hair of him.

"You won't," declared John Rafferty, to whom Cameron had given an account of his misadventure. "Once he got back to the cabin and saw those dead snakes, you can be certain that he lit out for parts unknown. Right now I bet he's puzzling himself gray-headed over how you did it."

"I'd have liked to remain in the vicinity of the cabin and possibly get a look at whoever he was bringing back with him, but I just didn't feel equal to it," Cameron said. "I wasn't in very good shape about then, and figured the best thing

I could do was get in the clear."

"You're right," agreed Rafferty. "You'd very likely have just ended up getting yourself killed. No telling how many the devil brought back with him."

"I wonder which it was, Fitch or Sterns?" Cameron observed reflectively.

"My guess would be Sterns, judging from what they told you about somebody being anxious to get certain information," Rafferty said. "That don't sound like Fitch. I figure all Fitch wants to do is drill a hole through you. He ain't overly bright and isn't given to working out slick schemes. Sterns is bright, plenty bright, and I calc'late he has something in mind that has to do with Prince Carl and his bunch. I think Sterns is a bit bothered over you getting chummy with the prince. And my advice is to watch out for him. He's more dangerous than Fitch, because he's smarter."

Cameron was inclined to agree with the saloonkeeper and resolved that he would not again be caught off his guard.

CHAPTER XV

In Carlshafen the weather continued vile. The days were blazing, the nights hot and humid. Cameron had trouble sleeping, and rising to face the day was something to shrink from. He congratulated himself on forcing Mary to remain in New Braunfels. There was great suffering in the shack town that housed the immigrants, and Cameron's feeling of foreboding intensified. He was thankful when another of the pitifully inadequate wagon trains got under way, and he returned to Carlshafen again dreading what he might find there.

However, except that more colonists had arrived during his absence—von Meusebach had not—there was little change in conditions.

And then the terror struck!

In one of the shacks a man became violently
ill. Cameron heard about it and at once visited
Doctor Cooper.

Doc, as everybody called him, was a typical
frontier doctor who had arrived in Carlshafen
from San Antonio about six months before. He
was old, but the wanderlust still gripped him.
He had practiced in a score of Texas communities and in other states and enjoyed a wide-flung
and excellent reputation.

"Wouldn't be surprised if I'll be following
you soon," he had told Cameron when the latter
announced his intention of heading west. "Sure
I'm building up a nice practice here, but I can't
stay in one place too long. Always hanker to see
what's on the other side of the next hill."

When they reached the shack where the suf-
ferer lay, Doc peremptorily ordered Cameron
to wait outside.

"I'll call you if I need you," he said.

Cameron waited, and it was a long wait. When
Doc finally reappeared his face was grim.

"Come on to the office," he said abruptly. "I
want to talk to you."

When they reached the office, Doc waved
Cameron to a chair, sat down himself and, with-

out speaking, began to stuff his old cherry-wood pipe with tobacco.

"Well, what is it?" Cameron asked. "Cholera? Yellow jack?"

The old doctor seemed to hesitate before replying, puffing on his pipe for several moments.

"Rance," he said at length, "I'm not sure what it is. There are certain symptoms of cholera, others reminiscent of yellow fever, still others that are not typical of either disease." He hesitated again, puffing hard. He removed the pipe from his mouth and continued.

"A strange thing to say, but what it calls to my mind most is a long and detailed description I once read of the old sweating sickness, or miliary fever, that was epidemic in the 15th and 16th centuries, often wiping out whole villages. It was very deadly in Britain and especially so in Germany. But sweating sickness is a disease that is supposed to have been practically extinct for centuries.

"Well, one thing is certain," Doc said grimly. "The man is going to die!"

The man did die, during the night, and next day there were three more cases of sickness, each marked by pyrexia, profuse sweats, and an eruption of miliary vesicles.

"Go tell Rosenthal," Doc said. "And locate Black Pete; I think we're going to need him."

Black Pete was a big colored man who had recovered from both cholera and yellow fever and considered himself immune from the diseases, and incidentally wasn't scared of disease or anything else. He had handled the disposal of plague victims in other communities. For it was agreed that the greatest danger of infection was from the bodies of the dead.

"Okay, Boss, I'll take over," Black Pete agreed when Cameron approached him where he was working on the waterfront. "Only I got to have a quart of whiskey each day; that kills the bugs."

"Get it from Rafferty," Doc snorted when Cameron mentioned Pete's condition. "The stuff he sells will kill anything. An innocent stranger who smelled one of his corks was crippled for life."

There was plenty of work for Black Pete to do in the days that followed, for the terror struck again and again and again. Men, women and children died, and Black Pete carted off the bodies and prepared them for burial.

Most of the Carlshafen people gave the shack town a wide berth, but Cameron, Papa Rosenthal, John Rafferty and some others helped Doc do what he could to relieve the sufferings of those stricken.

"If it wasn't for you fellows the death toll would be much higher," Doc declared. "I only hope none of you come down with it. There goes Pete with another load."

And then one day Black Pete approached Cameron in Rafferty's place, where he was pausing from his labors for a drink and something to eat.

"Boss," he said, I'm whupped. "There are too many of them for me to handle. In some of those tents and shacks there ain't nobody left alive, and some of the corpses are getting mighty ripe. Do you think you could hire somebody to help me?"

Cameron stood up, hitching his gun belt a little higher.

"I'll help you," he said briefly. "Let's go."

"Rance, you aren't going into those pest holes!" protested Rafferty. "You'll catch it sure. Everybody knows you can't handle a body without catching it."

"If I catch it, I'll catch it," Cameron replied, adding, "but I don't think I will. Come on, Pete."

Cameron quickly realized that Pete had not exaggerated when he'd said some of the bodies were getting mighty ripe. In many cases decomposition had already set in and often was well under way. The stench in the dark hovels was frightful and made Cameron sick.

"There are too many for us to try to bury them," he told Pete. "We'll pack them out and stack them over by that big oak tree. Then we'll drench them with oil and burn them; it's the only thing to do."

He gently informed the colonists of his intention, which was received for the most part in stoical silence. Men who had not yet been stricken offered to lend a hand, but Cameron declined their help.

"I think Pete and I are fairly safe," he explained, "but you folks are vulnerable, and there's no sense in you taking any risk you don't absolutely have to. Pete and I can handle the chore."

As the heap of bodies, some of them in horrible condition, grew, a crowd from Carlshafen watched from a safe distance, gradually edging closer as morbid curiosity overcame fear.

"The chance Cameron's taking!" a big cowhand rumbled. "Everybody knows if you touch the carcass of a feller who's died from the infernal plague you'll catch it. Gents, I'm taking my hat off to a man with guts!"

A man pushed his way to the front and stood watching Cameron and Pete at their grisly task. It was Mark Sterns. He held a cloth drenched with a carbolic solution to his nose and mouth. He removed the cloth for a moment and grinned, a grin of malicious satisfaction.

A flame of wrath enveloped Cameron. He bounded forward, seized Sterns by the shirt front, shook him till his teeth rattled and hurled him headlong into the pile of bodies. Sterns landed on his face, plowing through corruption. He screamed, a high-pitched cackling scream of utter terror. He tried to rise, slipped and wallowed in putrescence. Still screaming, he scrambled to his feet and ran blindly, clawing at his eyes and mouth. Head down he rushed, and struck head on the massive trunk of the great oak tree. He rebounded, spun around like a top and fell. For a moment his boot toes beat a queer, muffled tattoo on the ground and then were still. He lay on his side, his limbs drawn up, and his head screwed around at a hideously unnatural angle, so that his glazed eyes seemed to be looking straight over his own shoulder.

Cameron gazed down at the corpse. "Snapped his neck like a rotten stick," he observed to Pete. "Guess the good Lord knew what He was about when He grew that tree right where He did. Come on; we've got work to do."

The awestruck crowd stood silent, nobody offering to touch the body. Cameron heard a few mutters running through the front ranks:

"Busted his own neck!" "Guess he had it coming." "Never was no good." "Uh-huh, reckon it saved a good rope, sooner or later."

Such was Mark Sterns' requiem as sung by those who had known him.

Finally the exhausting task was finished. Black Pete fetched cans of oil. They drenched the dreary heap and set it afire. The watchers backed farther away as a thick column of black smoke rose in the still air.

"What about that one?" asked Pete, jerking his thumb toward where Mark Sterns lay. "Shall we burn him, too?"

"No," Cameron decided, glancing at the crackling pyre. "Over there is all that's left of good and decent people. No reason for them to be contaminated. We'll dig a hole and dump him in."

They proceeded to do so. Doc Cooper appeared as the last shovel of earth dropped on the low mound.

"All right, Rance," he ordered. "Come on over to the office and I'll douse you with everything I've got; maybe that'll keep the plague away from you."

Cameron was too utterly weary and heartsick to argue. In the doctor's office he was thoroughly fumigated.

"That ought to do it if anything will," Doc said.

"Doc," Cameron replied as he rolled a cigarette, "I don't believe I'll catch it."

"I don't believe you will, either," was the unexpected answer. "It isn't good science and it isn't good medicine to say so, but I've noticed that one who doesn't believe he will catch a disease and doesn't worry and fret about it doesn't catch it, although folks all around him do. Maybe the mind plays a stronger part in such matters than we ken."

"Doc, it is true, is it not, that fear, worry and nervousness tend to lower bodily resistance to disease?" The doctor nodded.

"And there may be your answer," Cameron concluded.

"Maybe," Cooper conceded, "but somehow I believe there's more to it than that! Hard to tell just what goes on in the citadel of the mind and how strong its effect on the body. Saint Paul said, 'They shall take up serpents and shall not be harmed.' Well, I've known folks who believed in what Paul said and handled snakes, and didn't get bitten. They were convinced the snakes wouldn't harm them, and they didn't. The Hopi Indians play with rattlers in the course of their tribal rituals and never get fanged."

"I do not think the problem is a very obscure one, and the answer's fairly obvious," Cameron said. "Snakes are not normally vicious creatures; they strike only when frightened, irritated or nervous. The Hopis, and others who handle snakes, are not afraid of them and consequently are not nervous. Fear and nervousness very likely communicate to the creatures just as they do to horses. If the handler's not nervous, the snake remains placid also."

"An ingenious and fairly logical conclusion," Cooper admitted. Once again he shot a curious glance at Cameron.

"You have considerable education, haven't you, son?" he commented.

Cameron laughed deprecatingly. "Not a great deal," he replied. "But I did manage to get in a couple of years at the University before I left Virginia on account of the feud."

"What did you plan to study?"

"Medicine," Cameron smiled.

"The devil you did!" Doc ejaculated. "And now you're a cowhand."

Cameron shrugged. "When one cannot get the moon, one has to be satisfied with sixpence," he replied.

Doc Cooper's glance became speculative. "How old are you?" he asked abruptly.

"Twenty-six."

"Then you're still plenty young enough," Doc declared. "I understand you plan to go back with Rivercomb, as his range boss. You'll have lots of spare time on your hands. Tell you what: right here I've got one of the best medical libraries in the state. Why not start reading medicine?

You can accompany me on cases and assist in surgical operations when I have to perform any. Stick with me and I'll make a doctor of you. What do you say?"

"Doc," Cameron replied, "I'll do it. I'll admit I don't hanker to follow a cow's tail all the rest of my life. I'll do it, and thanks loads for the offer."

"Then that's settled," said Cooper. "Come on; let's go over to Rafferty's for a drink and a bite to eat."

As they walked to the saloon, Doc suddenly chuckled. "I've a notion Mark Sterns was dead before he bumped into that tree," he observed. "Bet an autopsy would show he died of a heart attack induced by fright rather than from a busted neck. A case of retributive justice. If he'd done the right thing and provided transportation for those people as fast as they arrived here, all this wouldn't have happened, including his own come-uppance. Funny how things work out, but give 'em time and they usually work out right."

The plague continued to ravage the colony, with no signs of abatement. Finally a group of the elders came to Cameron.

"*Herr* Cameron," said one, an old man with

a white beard, who spoke halting English, "we leave here."

"Where will you go?" Cameron asked.

"To New Braunfels."

"But how?" Cameron protested. "We can't possibly transport all of you with the few vehicles we have at our command."

"We will walk," the oldster said.

"Walk! It's nearly two hundred miles over the roughest country."

"Better to die walking than to sit here and die rotting," the old man replied.

"You may be right," Cameron conceded. "Well, I'll ride with you and do what I can to help."

"You are a good man, *Herr* Cameron," the old man said, "to do so much for strangers."

Cameron's quick smile flashed in his bronzed face. "When affliction strikes there is no such thing as strangers," he said gently. "I'll go and talk to Papa Rosenthal."

CHAPTER XVI

Two days later the march began. The wagons were sent on ahead, loaded with as many children and very old people as they could accommodate, a pitiful few in contrast to the throng for whom there was no room.

Only the desperately ill were left behind in Carlshafen, with a few of the hale to care for them. North by west wound the long, slow-moving column, and with it marched an awful trinity—hunger, exhaustion, and disease. For the terror continued to strike, again, and yet again.

Day by day the colonists trudged doggedly on, under the blazing sun, under the unfeeling stars. Progress was discouragingly slow and the distance great indeed, but none spoke of turning back; none faltered as long as strength to move remained.

Rance Cameron never slept. Gaunt, hollow-eyed, haggard, he toiled ceaselessly to mitigate the suffering of the few to whom his hand could extend. At times he would carry a child in his arms for hours. At others he would walk weary miles while some exhausted man or woman rode the great blue horse that seemed to understand. Never, so long as life should last, would he forget the scenes he witnessed in the course of that terrible trek across the Texas plains. Old men falling by the wayside, rising to stagger on and fall again. Babies gasping out their lives between their blue lips. Stony-faced women whose eyes held no more tears to weep. In Cameron's black hair were threads of silver that had not been there before.

The wagons rolled down from New Braunfels, loaded with food, which helped a little, and with scarcely an hour of rest for men or horses rolled back again, crammed with those most desperately in need. The bearded, bleary-eyed teamsters, rocking on their seats with fatigue, cursed the soul of dead Mark Sterns and reserved a few choice expletives for the tardy Baron von Meusebach who, they felt, might have relieved the situation somewhat. Not until much later was the reason for the baron's delay explained—a smashed rudder and a ship drifting helplessly before the wind.

The march resumed, a dreary, endless treadmill of suffering and sorrow. Now the weaker were succumbing fast, and the strong were swiftly growing weak. Each day was a day of mourning, each night a dark fear of the morrow.

In grim silence the colonists buried their dead, with only a muttered prayer for the soul's repose as the last shovel of earth fell. Then again the never-ceasing onward shuffle, without a backward glance at the bare, brown mound stark and lonely under the sun.

How many died in Carlshafen and during the dreadful struggle through the wilderness? Nobody knows for sure. Some authorities say eight hundred, others no less than three thousand. Doubtless neither figure is correct, but the graves, now grass-grown, that mark that Trail of Tears are many!

Cameron lost all track of time. Carlshafen was a pain-filled eternity behind, New Braunfels another frightening eternity ahead. The hours were fiery spokes in a slowly turning wheel of torment without beginning and without end.

There were periods when his fever-freighted mind wondered dully if they were doomed to wander ceaselessly through a bleak desolation till the River of Time ran over the edge of the world and was lost beyond the sun.

At long last, under a sky of cloudless blue, the wooded slopes fell away and New Braunfels lay before them, nestling under the fort on the hill. Before sundown the last weary marcher was housed in comfort.

Cameron slept the clock around and awoke much his normal self. He found all bustle and orderly confusion in the town where permanent dwellings were being erected for the newcomers.

Still the terror struck and more died, but here its blows were weaker and the scourge retreated in defeat, and New Braunfels knew peace. Cameron made preparations to return to Carlshafen.

"There are still some more to come," he told Mary, "but I think we will be able to handle them without much trouble. Then we can get married and settle down on the Rocking R.

"I understand," he added, "that immigrants from other countries are also going to pass through Carlshafen—everybody is calling it Indianola now. I predict Indianola is going to become a very important port, which will be good for the cattle business in the section."

Cameron accompanied the wagon train when it left New Braunfels. He was in no hurry and decided that he deserved a rest. In fact, after the terrible journey north, the slow ride back to the coast was in the nature of a pleasure jaunt. The horses were in poor condition, and Cameron insisted that they be allowed to choose their own gait while recovering their strength.

In consequence it took much more than the average time to complete the trip. Day after day they journeyed on leisurely across the endless prairie, watching the sun rise, watching it mount high, watching it sink again. Night after night they ate their simple food with appetite and slept beneath the glittering stars till a new dawn broke in glory.

Cliff Hardy shook his head sadly over the seemingly endless procession of graves that marked the trail.

"Old Texas is sure salted blue with bones," he mused aloud. "Well, bones nourish the soil and help make things grow. And folks like these who die are doing their share to make her what she'll be some day."

When they reached Carlshafen they found that more immigrants had arrived during their absence. But Rosenthal and his assistants had contrived to better conditions. With the thinning of the population, more space was available, and they were able to avoid unsanitary crowding and provide better shelter. And, as in New Braunfels, the plague had apparently spent itself.

"Ended as suddenly as it began," Doc Cooper told Cameron. "Another characteristic of sweating sickness. One day we had four new cases, the next none. Several days later we had one, and after that none at all. I don't think we need fear a recurrence."

With the ghastly scenes of that terrible march fresh in his mind, Cameron fervently hoped the doctor was right.

Cameron contacted Jim Rivercomb in the Best Chance the following evening. The ranch owner shook hands and congratulated him on his safe return.

"It was more than I hoped for when you left," he said. "You sure took a chance, going into those hovels and packing out the bodies, some of 'em in a shape that would have turned a buzzard's stomach; and right on top of it, taking that trip to New Braunfels. Hardy told me that the second time the wagons came down to meet you, you looked like a jigger who'd been dead three days. Well, it 'pears like things are under control at last. Reckon you're pretty near ready to take over at the spread, yes? The job's waiting for you. Hardy is plumb anxious to pull out and start looking after his own holdings. How's the girl?"

"She's fine," Cameron told him. "Have you seen anything of Fitch?"

"Uh-huh," Rivercomb replied. "I've been keeping an eye on that hombre, hoping to catch him trying to pull something. So far, though, I ain't had no luck. He's been sticking close to his freighting business; got a good army contract, I understand. Yesterday evening, though, him and four of his hellions rode north, heading for San Antonio, I reckon. They had a pack mule with them. Bet you somebody over there catches it."

"Quite likely," Cameron agreed. "But they might just be going on a bust. I've a notion Fitch figures he'd better stay away from here for a while, till things sort of cool down."

"Wouldn't be surprised if you're right," Rivercomb conceded. "Ain't much doubt but that you scared the stuffings out of him that night. Besides, folks here might sort of look sideways at him after what he tried to pull, and he knows it. Fitch is a lot of things we could do without, but he ain't no fool. Just the same, I'm still willing to bet he pulls something around San Antonio. He always manages to keep in the clear, even though the other jiggers with him end up eating lead. But he'll slip sooner or later; his kind always does. And I sure hope I'm handy to pull on the rope."

Cameron and Rosenthal had agreed that horses and drivers both needed a bit more rest, so it was decided, since things were going along fairly smoothly, that another train would not roll north till the following week. ·

"Surely by then the baron will have arrived and can take charge," Papa predicted hopefully.

Cameron hoped so, too; he was eager to take up his duties at the Walking R, where he could marry Mary and settle down to an orderly and peaceful existence.

After his talk with Jim Rivercomb, Cameron left the saloon and strolled about the town. A strange restlessness had taken hold of him, accompanied by a vague but unpleasant uneasiness. He wondered what could be back of Lije Fitch's sudden and mysterious ride north, leaving his freighting business in the hands of subordinates at a critical time; the Army stood for no foolishness and would instantly cancel a contract if performance was not up to par. There was something queer about it.

He tried to shake off the disquieting foreboding, but without success. He glanced at the sky. Overhead it was clear, with a gibbous moon strengthening as the daylight faded, but to the northwest was a slowly rising cloud bank, dark and ominous and threatening. He swore at his over-active imagination that read portent in a purely natural phenomenon.

Analyzing his feelings, he realized that they were not necessarily based on anything psychic or supernatural. There was a very earthy fact present: he was bothered about Lije Fitch and his unexplained ride north. Fitch was a synonym for trouble. And although he might very well be headed for San Antonio as Jim Rivercomb surmised, he *had* ridden in the direction of New Braunfels. And Cameron could not get the incident of the pack mule out of his mind. If the bunch was headed for San Antonio and a bit of diversion, why the devil would they take a pack mule along?

Finally Cameron gave up. His condition could be remedied only by action. He was rested and so was his horse. He got the rig on Smoke, filled his saddle pouches with provisions, and without announcing his intention to anybody, rode north.

He rode at a steady pace and not too swiftly. It was wise to conserve his horse's strength, on the assumption that an emergency might arise when he would need everything the big moros had to give. Fitch was well ahead of him, but he reasoned that if the devil really had some skulduggery in mind, he would be careful not to exhaust his mounts beforehand. Yes, it was logical to assume that Fitch would take it easy.

He decided to do his riding at night, when he stood less chance of being observed, and took the precaution to skirt Victoria. He rode until dawn flushed the eastern sky, then made camp in a thicket beside a trickle of water. He lighted a small fire of dry wood, confident that the smoke would not be noticed in the morning mist, and cooked a meal, including food he would eat cold before resuming his ride at nightfall. Smoke made out okay on the luxuriant grass carpeting the floor of the little cleared space.

The darkness of the fourth night out found Cameron little more than twenty-five miles from New Braunfels, and at about midnight he neared the sleeping town. He was perhaps a mile from the slope of the hill on which the fort stood when he heard a distant crackle of gunfire. He jerked Smoke to a halt and sat listening. Two more shots sounded, seemingly from somewhere in the air, and then came silence.

"Trail, Smoke, trail!" he shouted, and sent the great moros charging for the slope. Across the level the blue horse sped, clattering through the silent streets. He reached the slope, toiled up it. In the fort, lights were flashing, and there came, thin with distance, the sound of a woman's scream.

Gritting his teeth, Cameron urged the horse to do his utmost. The moros responded gallantly, and scant minutes later Cameron halted him in front of the fort, hurling himself from the saddle while the horse was still in motion. He raced up the steps and into the building. In the great hall men and women were running about wildly in all stages of undress. Mary came flying from the back of the building.

"Rance!" she screamed. "Oh, thank goodness you're here! They killed Johan!"

Following the sobbing girl, Cameron hurried to the room in the back of the fort where Johan slept. It was a shambles. Three dead men lay on the floor. Two had been shot, the third's torso was twisted about, his glazed eyes bulged, and on his hard-featured face was stamped an awful look of agony and terror.

Johan lay on a bed to which he had been lifted. His face was livid, his eyes closed, and he breathed in stertorous gasps, blood frothing his lips. Henry hovered over him, muttering unintelligibly.

Cameron strode forward and knelt beside the dying man. Johan opened his eyes and smiled wanly.

"Always when needed you are present," he whispered.

"Can you tell us what happened?" Cameron asked as he opened Johan's shirt to bare his breast. There were two blue holes just above the heart.

"They burst in, five of them, with weapons in

their hands," Johan whispered. "He who led was a big man with glittering black eyes, a growth of short beard and a long chin. 'Where's the stuff?' he demanded. I knew that he meant the gold that is here in my room. I seized my pistols and shot two. The big man shot me twice, but before I fell I grappled with a third and broke his back across my knee. The others fled."

"A big man with black eyes and a long chin," Cameron repeated. "Get hot water and bandages," he called over his shoulder.

"You can do nothing," Johan gasped. "I have seen such wounds too often. I am filling up inside, fast. The pain, it is not too bad, *Gott sei dank*. But you can do nothing."

Cameron knew he was right; Johan had but a few minutes to live. He leaned close to catch any last words he might utter. Johan lay silent, his eyes closed, the hard gasps of his breathing slowly lessening. Abruptly he opened his sea-blue eyes and smiled again. A breath of sound seeped past the blood bubbles on his lips:

"Hoch der Vaterland!" And he was dead, dying as befitted a gentleman and a soldier.

Rance Cameron rose to his feet. His eyes were terrible, his face like flint, but when he spoke his voice was singularly soft and quiet.

"I want something to eat and coffee," he told Mary. "Henry, please see to my horse. Give him a good rubdown and a helping of oats, and water with a little whiskey in it. I'll be needing him soon."

Mary Stewart gazed at him, her eyes great dark pools of fear.

"You are going to ride after those men?" she faltered, her lips stiff.

"Of course," Cameron replied.

She did not plead or argue, knowing it would be useless, but hurried to provide him with all he needed.

As he ate, Cameron added a word of explanation. "I blame myself for what happened," he said bitterly. "I should have realized that Sterns, familiar with the Prince's habits and his intentions, would have given Fitch the lowdown on how things stood here. He would have known that Prince Carl would leave the gold behind. Doubtless the two hellions planned the raid, waiting till the prince had departed and the fort was practically unguarded. After Sterns was killed, there was even greater incentive for Fitch to make a try for the gold—he wouldn't have to share it with Sterns. Well, he didn't get it, but I wish Johan had let him have it. Yes, I should have anticipated something like what happened and taken precautions. So now it's up to me to even the score."

Again Mary uttered no word of remonstrance. When the moment came, she bade him a cheerful goodbye and hurried to consult with Henry.

Three hours after his arrival at the fort, the great blue horse forged steadily southward through the night. Once again a feuding Cameron of Calvert Valley was riding the vengeance trail.

And many miles behind rode a man who sat his horse in soldierly fashion, and a girl whose face was white and strained and whose lips moved in silent prayer.

CHAPTER XVII

Cameron did not push his horse, for he had no hope of overtaking the quarry on the trail. Fitch and his companion had a head start, and besides, they would very likely take some other route to Carlshafen. They wouldn't want to be seen riding from New Braunfels after what had happened there. He felt confident that Fitch would head for the port. He would think that it would be virtually impossible to pin the killing on him. Nobody but Johan had gotten a glimpse of him, and no doubt he assumed that Johan had been instantly killed. And of course he had no way of knowing that he, Cameron, had arrived in New Braunfels when he had. Carlshafen was the logical place for him to head. There was no hurry; Cameron let Smoke choose his own gait.

But the great moros traveled swiftly even

when not exerting himself, and Mary and Henry were never able to catch up.

Cameron arrived at Carlshafen in mid-afternoon. He stabled his horse and repaired to the Best Chance for a drink and something to eat. He was in no hurry. Fitch was either in Carlshafen or he wasn't; Cameron believed he was.

Rafferty and Jim Rivercomb were standing at the far end of the bar when Cameron entered the saloon. He nodded to them but did not speak, crossing to a table and sitting down. Rafferty and Rivercomb nodded back and exchanged glances. Apparently they sensed that something out of the ordinary was in the wind.

Cameron ate slowly, had a drink and smoked a cigarette. Then he got up and walked over to where Rivercomb and Rafferty stood.

"Fitch in town?" he asked.

Again the pair exchanged glances. "Yes, he's in town, down at the LaVaca, or was a little while ago," Rivercomb replied.

"Okay," Cameron said. "I'm going down to the Lavaca."

"Rance, what's up?" Rafferty asked.

"It's a showdown, John," Cameron replied simply.

"All right," said the saloonkeeper, taking down his Sharps rifle from the rack behind the bar. "We'll go with you. I think one of Fitch's hellions is with him," he added meaningly.

"Just as you wish," Cameron agreed. "Let's go!"

A hush fell over the Lavaca when Cameron entered. Rivercomb and Rafferty instantly fanned out on either side. Cameron walked slowly forward and paused about six paces from where Lije Fitch stood. He eyed the freighter in silence.

"Well, what do *you* want?" Fitch blustered nervously.

Cameron still regarded him in silence, his hands hanging by his sides. Then he spoke.

"Fitch, you know why I'm here. The man you shot at New Braunfels is dead. Fill your hand!"

But Lije Fitch shrank back, his face whitening. "I wouldn't have a chance," he mumbled. "Everybody knows you're chain lightning with that new-fangled iron of yours. And you've got six shots to my one."

Cameron eyed him for a moment in silent contempt. "All right," he said, "we'll even things up. Jim, you've got a single-shot pistol. Give it to me. Be sure it's in working order."

Without speaking, Rivercomb drew the weapon. He examined the priming, passed it to Cameron, who took it, his eyes never leaving Fitch, and let it hang loosely by his side.

"Fill your hand, Fitch," he repeated. "Somebody give the word to fire."

"I'll give it," said Rafferty as Fitch slid his gun from its sheath. Rafferty cocked the Sharps.

"And anybody who horns in or makes a wrong move gets an ounce of lead through his guts," he added. "You two ready? Fire!"

The two pistols leaped forward and exploded as one. Rance Cameron staggered, his knees buckled under him, and he slumped to the floor.

Fitch also staggered, but he stood firmly erect, while the smoking pistol dropped from his hand and thudded on the boards. He raised the hand slowly, uncertainly, to his lips. He looked at the fingers, and an expression of horrified disbelief distorted his features. He tried to speak, but blood gushed from his mouth in a torrent, drowning the words. With a gasping gurgle, he pitched forward and lay still.

Rafferty and Rivercomb rushed to Cameron and knelt beside him. As they turned him over on his back, Doc Cooper came shouldering through the shouting crowd and joined them. He ripped open Cameron's shirt to reveal a blue hole in his left breast, from which a slow bubble of blood rose and fell.

"High up, anyhow, thank goodness!" he muttered. "But it's a wind wound—pierced the lung —and bad. All right, you fellows, get a shutter or a table top or something and pack him over to the office. I'll do what I can. Fitch? Dead as a door nail. If he wasn't, I'd give him something that would poison him. All right; let's go."

Rance Cameron remembered nothing of the two days that followed, days of semi-consciousness and delirium. On the morning of the third day after the fight in the Lavaca he awoke, weak but sane. Gradually he realized there was someone on the chair beside him. It was Mary, dozing. He raised a hand, marveling at the effort it took to do so, and touched her hair. Instantly she was awake. A glad light filled her eyes.

"Oh, my darling, you've come back to me!" she murmured, and broke into uncontrollable sobbing.

Doc Cooper came hurrying in, Henry at his heels. "So!" he exclaimed. "Decided not to make a day of it, eh? Which was more than I expected at one time. Well, you can thank *her* that you're alive right now. She's never left you, hasn't slept and we could hardly get her to eat. How you feeling now, Mary?"

But Mary didn't answer. Her head was back, her arms around Cameron's neck.

"Sound asleep, and no wonder," chuckled Doc. "Pick her up, Henry, and we'll put her to bed. She'll be okay in about twelve hours. Now I expect this gent can use a little broth. I'll have Rafferty send some over in a jiffy. You darn loco young fool, giving that murderous sidewinder an even break! But I'm proud of you!"

From then on, Cameron's recovery was rapid; he was sitting up the next day.

"Yes, the baron arrived," Mary told him. "He was delayed by a near-shipwreck. He came and stood by the bed and said a prayer for you, and he promised to visit us soon. Got well fast, darling; we've got lots of things to do."

A week later she announced, "Mr. Rivercomb is going to drive us out to the ranch tomorrow; Doctor Cooper says it's all right."

"First we're driving up to Victoria," Cameron said.

"Why?"

"They've got a preacher at Victoria."

The evening of the second day, Rance Cameron and his pretty young wife stood in the doorway of their own home, the little house not far from the big Walking R ranchhouse. Mary gazed into the sunset, her eyes dream-filled.

"What you thinking about, honey?" he asked.

She turned her head slowly and smiled up at him.

"Cradles!"

Leslie Scott was born in Lewisburg, West Virginia. During the Great War, he joined the French Foreign Legion and spent four years in the trenches. In the 1920s he worked as a mining engineer and bridge builder in the western American states and in China before setting in New York. A barroom discussion in 1934 with Leo Margulies, who was managing editor for Standard Magazines, prompted Scott to try writing fiction. He went on to create two of the most notable series characters in Western pulp magazines. In 1936, when Standard Magazines launched *Texas Rangers*, Scott under the house name of Jackson Cole created Jim Hatfield, Texas Ranger, a character whose popularity was so great with readers that this magazine featuring his adventures lasted until 1958. When others eventually began contributing Jim Hatfield stories, Scott created another Texas Ranger hero, Walt Slade, better known as El Halcon, the Hawk, whose exploits were regularly featured in *Thrilling Western*. In the 1950s Scott moved quickly into writing book-length adventures about both Jim Hatfield and Walt Slade in long series of original paperback Westerns. At the same time, however, Scott was also doing some of his best work in hardcover Westerns published by Arcadia House; thoughtful, well-constructed stories, with engaging characters and authentic settings and situations. Among the best of these, surely, are *Silver City* (1953), *Longhorn Empire* (1954), *The Trail Builders* (1956), and *Blood on the Rio Grande* (1959). In these hardcover Westerns, many of which have never been reprinted, Scott proved himself highly capable of writing traditional Western stories with characters who have sufficient depth to change in the course of the narrative and with a degree of authenticity and historical accuracy absent from many of his series stories.